MW00768681

Alien in the Mirror

Homeworld: Book One

Published by The McNarn Group

Centralia, Washington

http://www.thoughtdairy.com/mcnarn

Text copyright © 2000 by Casey Lytle
all rights reserved

First printing, March 2000

Edited by Lorena Lytle and Michelle Lytle

Printed and bound in the United States by
Capitol City Press
116 Capitol Way North
Olympia, WA 98501
print@capitolcitypress.com
www.capitolcitypress.com

Library of Congress Card Number: 00-101427

ISBN 0-9678933-0-5

For everyone who's wondered if their parents are really from this planet.

Prologue
Olympia, Washington – Earth

This was bad. Officially completely bad. Everything was coming completely undone.

Hennesey gasped for breath; his shoes tapped on the pavement like the rapid ticking of a clock; he was running as fast as he could, but he wasn't catching up to the man. A half block ahead the man emerged from the shadow between streetlights, and darted into a crosswalk. Horns honked and tires squealed as cars swerved to avoid hitting him.

"No," Hennesey gasped, "No, don't get hit." How could the man run so fast? He was an old man, easily twice Hennesey's age, but he just kept running.

If I stop we may never see him again, Hennesey thought. Traffic was still stopped at the intersection as Hennesey ran through; drivers were still yelling at the old man who was almost a block away already.

"I'm not gaining on him," Hennesey said. The

people back in the van were watching and listening. Small jewels on Hennesey's glasses were sending pictures, a lion-head ring on his right hand was recording every sound. The pager on his belt contained a tracking chip, so they would know exactly where he was. It was standard issue and included a link to the Global Positioning Satellite so he would always know exactly where he was on the World Map. It was the one feature he would probably never need, but his little brother thought it was totally cool.

When the man reached the next corner he turned west, toward the Marina. Good and bad. He could only run another block before the street ended … but … the Marina.

A boat, Hennesey realized, he's got a boat over there. That's how he'll get away.

"He's going for the marina," Hennesey said as he raced around the corner. An older couple looked at him like he was crazy. Running as fast as he good, panting like an exhausted dog, and talking to himself.

Half a block away the street ended at the Marina. A boardwalk was lit with bright vapor lights designed to look like old-fashioned gas lamps. The man was standing at the railing, looking down on the moored boats swaying slightly on the dark water. He looked back, saw Hennesey, and hurried down the plank out of sight.

The mission briefing was replaying in Hennesey's head now. "Don't think … just do it," the commander had said, "they can feel your thoughts. Think of normal things. Boring things."

It was hard though. He was excited, and scared.

He tried thinking about his grocery list. He reached the railing and looked down. The man was running down the length of the dock, past the edge of the dock lights. As Hennesey watched, the man disappeared into the inky shadows.

The pager began to vibrate. It was the signal. Back-up was on it's way. It made him feel better; more confident, maybe a little braver. He raced down the plank onto the dock. The man was down there somewhere, in the shadows, waiting for a boat, or just standing there. Maybe he would be willing to talk.

Hennesey stepped past the last light. He slowed, walking cautiously into the shadow. "My name is Hennesey. I just want to talk to you. That's all. I'm unarmed," he held his hands in the air.

After several steps into the shadows he could see better. The dock ended thirty feet away. The man was standing at the very end, facing him.

"We mean no harm," Hennesey said, "we just want to talk."

The man was looking around calmly, scanning the boardwalk, as if making sure they were alone. Fear gripped Hennesey. A trap. The man pointed something at him, small, shiny. Not a gun …but …

A flash of brilliant white light. Like thousands of flashbulbs going off all at once. Hennesey felt dizzy. He could not see anything but bright white. I've been shot, he thought. This is what it's like to get shot. It continued for several seconds, then it was gone.

He suddenly bounced on his feet, as if someone

had been holding him down, then let go. The bright white light was now sunlight. The gentle sound of water lapping at the dock had turned into waves crashing on a beach. A warm breeze blew across his face, and clean, odorless air filled his lungs. He felt his feet slide a little. He wasn't standing on a dock now, he was on a beach. The man was no longer in front of him. His glasses were buzzing in his ear, they had lost contact with the van.

Shielding his eyes from the bright sunlight he pulled the pager off the clip and looked at the display. The Global Positioning Satellite should tell him where he was, but the screen simply said, "searching." That was odd. It should only do that if it could not find the satellite. That was impossible … unless …

He took his hands away from his eyes, blinking rapidly to adjust to the light. He needed to see his surroundings. Then he noticed the sky. It was not blue, not even a grey polluted haze. It was pale lavender. And floating high in the swirls of that odd color were the blinding bright orbs of two suns.

Chapter One

September was still considered summer, but Candy Tennison was certain she could feel the cold, dark, stormy days of Winter peering over her shoulder. It was the first day of the new school year and absolutely everything had gone wrong. Her brand new clock radio had not gone off on time, then three pair of nylons shredded before they were past the knee. In frustration she had hurled her new backpack onto the bed, ripping open a seam, spilling it's contents. That hurt. It meant she had to go back to the old pink backpack she had used last year. It was so outdated, so juvenile, so ... *seventh grade!"*

No nylons meant no summer dress, so she changed to a new yellow blouse and dark green cutoff overalls. Not the eye-catching *first day* look she was going for, but the way the morning was starting she would feel lucky not to get run over by the bus at the bus stop.

In the kitchen, her Dad had his head hung over a bowl of oatmeal. He seemed to be deep in thought. Her

9

Mom was acting like she was reading the newspaper, nervously tapping her long fingernails on the tabletop. Her brother Carl had already left for the bus stop a half hour ago; the high school students started an hour earlier. Candy scarfed a bowl of cereal, being careful to keep her mouth over the bowl and not let any milk splash onto her clothes. She spared a few glances at her parents, they would smile politely and nod, but they weren't very talkative. Usually the air would be full of her mother saying "Oh Willoughby, stop talking nonsense," and her dad would reply, "Arlia, it's not that simple," and it would go on and on.

But not this morning. They still seemed to be in that *nervous* mood they had been in almost all summer. She had hoped the beginning of the school year would snap them out of it. Return everyone to the same boring routine. After all, parents were supposed to be the one constant in your life right? The ones who *started* the boring routines and made you go through them day after day. Her and Carl were supposed to be the ones to change as they got older. Parents were never supposed to change … or act weird … or just nod at breakfast when they should be talking.

The thought vanished as she placed the empty bowl in the sink and felt cold wetness spread on a spot along her stomach. She screamed and jumped back. A leftover spill from Carl's instant breakfast was pooled on the edge of the sink. Chocolate. Now a big brown stain decorated the yellow blouse. She stomped her foot. "Mom!" she whined, pointing at the stain.

"Better change," Her mom said blankly. That wasn't

really the sort of parental advice Candy needed. Something more like. "Don't worry dear, that's just instant breakfast. In a couple minutes it'll fade and you'll never know it was there. And if it doesn't, we'll ground Carl for the whole year." Mornings like this helped convince her that there had to be some sort of guiding force to the Universe. Because this many bad things could not happen on the first day of school simply by coincidence.

So much for starting the school year with a fashion statement. She changed into a plain blue tee shirt under the short overalls. Whatever disaster befell this outfit between now and the first class wouldn't really matter.

"I'm the mist," she chanted, "I'm a cloud," it was something Carl had taught her over the summer. A little trick to cool down and get back in control when things were getting out of control.

It was chilly outside right now, but later it was supposed to get warm. That's what made it so hard to go back to school. Summertime sunshine and the smell of freshly cut grass. All the major ingredients to keep her from paying attention in class.

The air nipped at her lungs when she opened the front door. The tee shirt and cut-off overalls might not be such a good idea. She hesitated a moment. The way this morning was going, if she changed into something warmer the temperature would hit seventy by the time she reached the bus stop.

No, she wouldn't change … not again. She simply had to get to the bus stop, endure maybe ten minutes of chilly weather, then climb into the shelter of the bus and the moist sweaty heat of the other middle-school kids.

She leaned back through the door and grabbed a windbreaker. It was light and would roll up easily into her bag. A little fast walking for about a block, then she would stuff the jacket in the bag, and she would show up at the bus stop looking every bit the summer girl. There didn't seem to be much of a breeze; that was good. No need to tie back the shoulder-length locks. Her hair had lightened over the summer to a lighter blonde; her friends would accuse her of coloring it.

She closed the door quickly, before her parents noticed her hesitation. But of course they wouldn't. They were stuck to their chairs back in the kitchen. Whatever was bothering them it wasn't something they found important enough to talk to her or Carl about. Fine with her. But the next time they jumped on her about getting home late from Jan's ...

But ... she *had* been coming home late from Jan's, and they had not said anything about it. Part of her said it was because she was in Eighth Grade now and deserved more freedom, more respect. She was a young lady, not a little kid. But another part of her felt like she had been cast out into a cold world of responsibility. That part still wanted to be protected by Mom and Dad; still wanted to be told the right thing to do.

Not important now, she thought as she bounced down the steps and headed up the sidewalk. The cold air made everything seem clearer; more real. Taking a deep breath she felt the distance grow between her and the house. Maybe it was the walking, maybe it was the heat of her thoughts, but about half a block later the air didn't seem quite as cold. Her nose even seemed to warm up a bit. She took the jacket off and stuffed it into her bag, right next to her new Organizer, loaded with clean crisp paper and new pencils. The one thing which had not suffered a disaster so far this morning.

The bus stop was at the old Elementary School which she had attended from Kindergarten to Sixth Grade. A hundred-year-old school in the middle of the oldest neighborhood on the West Hills, just a few blocks from the southern end of Puget Sound. This part of Olympia was Small Town U.S.A. Cracked concrete streets and grassy tree-lined parkways.

Fifteen months ago she had graduated from that old brick building, it seemed like forever; like she was an entirely different person from the girl who had run out of those creaky paint-chipped doors, excited by being out of grade-school and headed for Middle School. It had been hard to believe she was a seventh grader. Now *seventh grader* sounded just as childish as *grade-schooler.*

The world changes a lot when you realize your parents don't know everything. When you realize they can be scared by things just as much as you. That's what seventh grade — and especially this last summer — had been for Candy. Seeing her parents act strange, and sometimes afraid. And her brother — who for years had been more of an adversary than a relative — was now a friend. Her best friend. He was someone she could talk to, and feel safe with. A protector. She still had her friends, but more of her home time this summer had been spent with Carl.

13

Talking about stuff. About what it was like for her in Middle School and for him in High School. He had a lot of good advice. Hot summer nights just walking around the neighborhood because neither of them could stand to watch Mom and Dad acting weird, pacing around the house as if something terrible was about to happen.

"You don't think they're going to get a divorce do you?" Candy asked nervously.

"No," he said, but he wasn't certain, "I never notice them fighting. Don't you have to argue a lot before you get a divorce?"

Candy shrugged her shoulders, "Jan's whole family was in counseling for a year before her parents got divorced."

"Dad's always hanging around the front window like he's expecting someone to show up."

For a while they suspected Dad was in some sort of trouble at work. Something that would show up on the news, then the police would come and take him away. That's the way Mom acted; like someone was going to come in and take everything away. Dad had a research job of some kind. He had an office downtown but also did a lot of work on the computer at home. Always typing something, always sending away long E-mails. Always a deadline for a report of some kind.

When they were little kids, Candy and Carl imagined Dad was a spy. Doing all sorts of secret things for the government. Over the summer they had laughed at those memories, but wondered if perhaps he really was involved in something government-related. Something bad. Something illegal.

They had talked about it so much that guessing became a game, and that made it a little less serious and less scary.

At the bus stop there were familiar faces standing out at the curb, and of course an entire new group of Seventh Graders. No doubt all of them were terrified of their first day of Middle School, but most were doing a good job of looking calm. It seemed a few were already joining the group of smokers under the cover of the bicycle racks. Tami Seltzer was already talking. She talked almost continuously, most of the time about nothing. Candy wondered what she did during the summer without kids her age to talk to. She was a big chat-room junkie on the computer. Their phone line had probably been busy all summer.

Candy loved the walk from the corner to the bus stop. This year she was an Eighth Grader. A Young Lady. No one was going to make smart cracks to her or hassle her or look down on her because they were older.

Last year the bus stop had been kind of a scary place because of the taunting of the smokers over by the bike rack. It had been weird enough seeing kids her age smoking. It was like walking into a different world … a weird world.

The smokers were like dragons, hanging back in the cave-like shade of the bike racks, breathing their fire, and roaring at the other kids. Mostly it was just teasing. A test of self-control. But sometimes teasing had turned to pushing, and Candy's fear would get the better of her and she would curl up and surrender like a little mouse. "That just makes you a target for next time," Carl had told her during the summer, "stand up to them and they're less likely to pick on you next time." He would drill her by playing the role of the bully — a role he had been good at all his life — and she would practice standing up to him. Maybe that was another reason they got along better now; by teaching her to stand up to the bullies, he was also teaching her to stand up to him.

"Nice bag, Barbie!" a voice cackled like a witch from the shadow of the bike racks. It was Wilma Jenkins, one of the eighth graders. Wilma hung out with the smokers all last year. She had scraggly black hair which never looked brushed. Her clothes were outdated and her skin was pale, like it was on the edge of turning into freckles. Candy had known her in grade-school, but not very well. She was not sure what had turned Wilma toward the smokers; she seemed to have a lot of anger inside. Normally she was pretty quiet, hiding behind the bigger girls, laughing as they pushed people around. But once the serious teasing started she would get brave, and with the support of the bigger girls she would yell, push, steal, and generally harass smaller and weaker kids just like the bigger girls did. It looked like this year she was comfortable stepping into the role of Lead Bully.

Well, she had picked the wrong person to start on. Candy was not the same girl who had been bullied at this bus stop last year … and besides, she was having a bad morning.

Last year she would have avoided looking at Wilma.

16

She would hurry nervously to her group of friends and try to hide among them, hoping Wilma would forget about her. This was probably what Wilma expected now. But this was not what Wilma got.

Candy slipped her bag off her shoulder and threw it toward her friends, then turned on her heels and marched straight toward Wilma, looking the dark-haired girl straight in the eye and not even blinking. This is what Carl had told her to do. "If you don't blink," he said, "it kind of makes you look crazy. That's good if you're in it with someone." Candy was taking long fast strides, looking like a bowling ball about to cream the pins. Wilma's eyes grew large and she took a step back without thinking. When she realized people were watching her she tried to put on a mean face.

"You want to start something with me *Wilma?*" Candy said, making the name sound like something to be ashamed of. "This is not the morning for it," she stopped less than six inches from Wilma's face. "But hey," she took a half step back and spread her arms, palms out as if inviting a fight, "if you want it, I'm dressed for it … Wil-Ma!" They stood staring at each other. Candy had still not blinked; Wilma was blinking like a crazy person. "Got something in your eye?" Candy asked. Then she turned and walked back to her friends.

Wilma said something, but Candy ignored it. Without skipping a beat she turned her attention to the girls standing curbside. "Jan! Nice outfit. Can you believe how cold it is?" She shrugged her shoulders and dipped into the group, paying no attention to the smokers laughing at Wilma.

"Nice tactic," Jan said. She was wearing lipstick for the first time and looked like she had tried some eyeliner then wiped it off and tried again. "That might shut her up, or it might cause us to get burning cigarette butts thrown at us." Jan was Candy's height, just over five and a half feet. Taller than average for an eighth grade girl, filling out but still trying to hide it beneath a baggy sweatshirt.

"Oh my gawd!" Tami yelled, "that was so cool! I can't believe it! You rock! It's like last year when Linda Buckingham and Lorrie Watkinson got into that fight behind the gym and Mister Finster tried to break it up when Lorrie was swinging her bag … "

Candy leaned toward Jan, if she stood here listening to Tami she would never get a chance to talk until after school. "Her buddies are all gone this year," Candy said, "and I don't think she's the leader type. And I get the feeling she's a little shaken up this morning. Must not like going back to school."

In the fifth grade Candy had developed the ability to guess people's moods. Most who heard about it teased her and didn't take it seriously, but her close friends considered it the Real Deal. It was something else her and Carl had in common. They could both do it. Not with each other, or with their parents, but when it came to other people they could both open up and feel what other people were feeling. It was kind of weird, kind of scary, but Candy had decided she was going to work on it this year; see how good she could get at it.

"She has to wait a couple hours between smokes," Jan grinned, "she'll drop from a nicotine fit during PE." She peeked at the smokers to make sure they were staying back there. "This is going to be a great year if they're that easy to put down."

"It won't be any fun if we don't get a chance to smack one of them," Amy Nottingham said. Amy was about Candy's height, with pouty eyes, dark eyebrows, full lips, and long curly black hair which hung down to the middle of her back. Her and Candy were good friends during the school year, but never managed to stay in touch during the summer. It was odd for Amy to talk about *smacking* someone. Candy got the feeling something was eating at her. She seemed a little angry and afraid at the same time.

Janae Headley, a short blonde eighth grader known as The Writer since fourth grade — when she kept a detailed diary of the entire year — leaned in cautiously. "I think they're scared of cops."

Jan and Candy looked puzzled. Janae tilted her head down the street. About a block away, sitting behind an old rusty Volkswagen Bug was a shiny black car. It's side and rear windows were tinted, making it hard to see inside, but barely visible were two men with white shirts and ties.

"They showed up a couple minutes before you," Janae said quietly, "they drove by kind of slow a couple times, spooked the smokers, then parked down there. If they're undercover cops they're not doing a very good job."

"Maybe it has something to do with Janet," Jan sug-

19

gested. Janet Sporinki had been in seventh grade with them last year. One day she didn't show up at school. Police came and talked to everyone at the bus stop and everyone at the school; they passed around a picture of a balding man with a goatee who none of them had ever seen before. Someone said it was her dad and he had taken her away somewhere to keep her from her mother. But no one would ever say for sure, and no one had seen Janet since. Candy and Carl had walked by her house a couple times during the summer. In July Janet's mother moved away, leaving the house dark and empty; a For Sale sign in the yard. In August new people moved in.

"I don't think so," Candy said. It was just a *feeling,* but she didn't want to say any more. It was just a black car with a couple guys in it. But for some reason she felt like they were watching her, and if they came any closer she should run like the wind and scream like a demon until *real* police showed up.

In the pit of her stomach she felt afraid. She wanted Carl here, telling her what he thought of the men in the car, and telling her everything would be alright. Had that car been driving around an hour earlier too? When Carl and the other High School kids stood here waiting for their bus? He would have noticed something like that. She would be sure to ask him later.

Suddenly there was a crowd pressing around her and she noticed the bus just a couple blocks away. A couple dozen middle-schoolers all trying to cram against the curb, fighting for a good position to get a good seat. This was the last stop before the Middle School so most of the good seats were already taken, except the back where the smokers would collect. No one wanted to get stuck back there.

Candy, Amy and Jan were the front three when the bus pulled up. The mob pushed them onto the bus once the doors opened. Amy scooted past Candy and got a window seat, Candy grabbed the aisle next to her, just five rows from the front. Jan slipped into the seat behind them. Candy was turning around to talk to Jan when something hard hit her in the cheek and knocked her head back.

"Ouch! Knock it off!" she cried as she turned. Wilma Jenkins was rubbing her elbow, giving Candy the evil eye.

"Keep your face out of my way!" Wilma hissed. She leaned down, ugly cigarette breath blowing across Candy's face, "or I might have to tear it off!"

Wilma had found her nerve again, or was being spurred on by her friends. Candy had the feeling it was a little of both. This is what Carl would call an "Uncle Mo" moment. The momentum between her and Wilma would turn one way or another. Candy felt a sliver of the same fear she had felt all last year. The fear which made her want to cry and run home to Mom. Her breath caught in her throat, her heart raced and she felt the beginnings of a tremble. Carl would be a good asset right now. "Don't fear," he would say, "just shovel it right back at her." She needed to find the courage and anger she had felt earlier.

Candy looked Wilma in the eye, and struggled not to blink, "Give it your best shot … Scrag!" she sneered. Wilma blinked, she started to open her mouth, then stopped, and suddenly she let the crowd of students carry her down the aisle toward the back. *Scrag* was a big insult … at least last year it was, and since this was the first day of school Candy figured it wasn't out of date yet. She was not sure exactly what *Scrag* meant, but it sounded like something you would say to someone who never washed their hair. So it fit Wilma perfectly.

Amy held up the Fist Of Triumph. Candy made a fist of her own and they knocked them together. "Way to go big sister!" Amy said. "And a New Age is born!"

Candy still felt the trembling, and her heart was still racing; it was a little hard to breathe straight. But under it all was a kind of rush of excitement. Like the feeling you have after getting off a roller coaster. It was good. She had "Uncle Mo" on her side. Carl would be proud.

Chapter Two

James Morlana imagined he was inside a drum. That's the noise his body made as it slammed against the metal locker doors. He was held by two sets of strong arms. "Pretty daring, Jimmy," Donny said. "Next time you take a swing make sure you've got some backup," his voice echoed off the concrete walls of *the bunker,* the locker area just a corridor away from the lunchroom. A Teacher had patrolled the area just minutes ago. No chance another one would be by soon enough to save him.

James was getting that tight feeling in his chest and dizziness in his head which came when he knew he was in trouble. Big trouble. He didn't need to be a mind reader to know Donny was ticked, and about to throw a punch. Probably more than one.

He was trying to brace himself for it, wondering where the first one would land. Stomach? Face? Hopefully not right in the nose. If he took a shot to the nose he would end up in the restroom for an hour mopping up blood with toilet paper shoved up his nose. But of course a good shot to the stomach might bring up breakfast; cereal and orange juice. Nothing too embarrassing. No big chunks. Still, it's hard to be cool when you're on your hands and knees in front of your locker staring at an orange pool of chewed breakfast.

Donny had his fist cocked, arm pulled back into position, ready for launch. James closed his eyes, he could almost feel his face going numb already.

"You going to punch him Donny?" a voice said. James opened his eyes. A few rows away stood Carl Tennison. His six-foot frame was gliding confidently toward them. His blue denim backpack was slung casually over his right shoulder, blue plaid outer shirt unbuttoned over a dark blue tee shirt. Not a slave to fashion, his jeans were just baggy enough without being ridiculous. He didn't look frightened, he didn't look angry or intimidating. He just looked curious. "Well?" he asked. "You two are holding him like you're about to do something."

Ronald Betts was holding James's right shoulder; he let go and took a step back. Donny didn't let go, but didn't take his eyes off Carl. "What's it to you? The guy took a swing at me, I'm just going to return the favor."

Carl grinned, "Fair enough," he said. "Doesn't look like he bloodied you up too much though."

"He missed," Donny sneered, "lucky for him or he'd need an ambulance by now."

"Ah," Carl said, as if Donny had just answered a question. Carl's locker was just a couple feet away. He stopped and casually spun his combination. He didn't look at Donny as he spoke. "So his swing missed. In that

24

case … if yours doesn't … neither will mine. James bleeds pretty easily. I imagine I'll have to pound you quite a bit to spill the same amount of blood."

Donny looked at Carl for a second, like he wanted to stare him down. But Carl didn't look back. "Hmphh!" Donny spat. He gave James a final shove against the locker and then turned away, "You pick losers for friends Tennison," he said. He disappeared around a corner with Betts on his heels.

"Thanks," James said, "you've got a lot of guts standing up to them like that."

Carl laughed. "Me? All I did was talk. You're the one who actually took a swing at him. I don't know if I'd call that guts, or suicide."

"He was calling me Jimmy," James said, "it just ticked me off."

"A lot of people are called Jimmy," Carl said, "it's not worth taking a swing at someone for."

"I know." James said meekly.

"They only say it 'cause they know it'll get to you."

"I know."

"Stacie Adams calls you Jimmy. I don't see you taking swings at her."

"I know."

"I know, I know," Carl mocked. "You always say that, but I don't think you really do know. Ever since grade-school every bully has known the trick to getting under your skin and making you throw a tantrum. You've got to brush it off and move along. And if it's those guys again," pointing after Donny, "don't take a swing, okay?"

25

"Okay."

"Next time you're in a situation like that you'll have two choices. Getting punched by them, or slapped around by me."

"Okay." James said, but Carl knew he had as much chance of getting through to James as he did talking to a rock. His words were just washing away. And just like a wave over a rock it would take hundreds, maybe thousands of years to have any noticeable effect.

"What's so bad about being called Jimmy anyway?"

"I just don't like it."

"So the next time Stacie asks about you, I should tell her you hate her because she calls you Jimmy?"

"That's different," he began meekly, then his eyes lit up, "she asks about me?"

Carl shook his head, pulled a book out of his locker. Something was itching, not on his body, but in his head. Like a strong feeling. Like when you know you forgot something but can't remember what. This was a little different. A presence. It was to his right, at the end of the row of lockers; maybe thirty feet away. He concentrated on it and it became clearer; stronger. Without looking he knew it was one of those people. Pretty daring of them to show up right here by the lockers. He closed his locker, then turned his head very slowly and deliberately toward the person. It was a man in a suit and tie, wearing sunglasses. It would be impossible for someone to stand out more than that. Carl locked his eyes on the dark plastic of the man's sunglasses and stared him down. He could feel the man's tension rise and then a sudden panic. The man turned quickly away and fled toward the cafeteria.

Since the end of last year Carl and Candy had been shadowed by men and women just like that. He had seen them driving through the neighborhood, wandering behind them at the mall, sitting in the back row at the movies. He had ignored them until now. But he was done ignoring them. It had to have something to do with what was bothering Mom and Dad, and he was going to find out.

At first, when he realized they were following him, he had been afraid. What did they want, what were their intentions? Later, when they were still following but making no moves to contact them he became curious. Now he was simply becoming angry. They were upsetting his life, making his parents weird, and making him uncomfortable and a little tense every time he turned a corner or saw a dark car driving by. Candy had said nothing about it, so she probably had not seen them yet, and he wasn't about to worry her by pointing them out.

"Carl?" James said, "You know that guy?"

"No." He had not noticed it before, but even though the man was gone, Carl could still sense his feelings. Fear, and flight. He even had a sense of where the man was; running through the lunchroom, heading for the nearest exit. Carl sprinted after him. He felt certain there was no danger to him here in the school. By chasing the man maybe he could scare them a little, shake them up, maybe chase them away completely.

He rose from the bunker into the lunchroom just as the double metal doors at the opposite end were closing. Everyone was looking that direction as if someone with two heads had just leapt from the kitchen and rushed out. Carl ran through the crowd, a few upperclassmen spat some remarks at him, he didn't listen. When he went out the doors he saw a black car pulling away.

"Mister Tennison?" a teacher had followed him to the door, "is there a problem?"

"Uh … " Carl was going to back down, but here was an opportunity, "that man," he pointed toward the black car, "was trying to get into the lockers … did you see him?"

"Yes I did," the teacher said curiously, "do you know him?"

"No. I was down by the lockers and saw him going down a row trying all the locks, like he was trying to get into a locker."

The teacher looked toward the black car. "Did you get the license number?"

"No."

"Well … good work Carl. I'll report this right away."

Carl grinned, and returned to the lunchroom. There you go, he thought, see how they like being watched, and maybe followed. The school would take something like this seriously, and the next time that black car showed up there would probably be police showing up soon after.

Candy was in the middle of second period math; the class she despised. And the only class with windows facing away from the school. Windows with green grass outside, and trees. Later in the day the groundskeeper would be mowing, and the smell of freshly cut grass would be mixing with the perfume of the evergreens being carried by a gentle warm breeze. And worse yet, about a mile through those trees was The Mall. How could anyone be expected to concentrate on a warm summer day so close to The Mall?

She found things to enjoy in every other class, even history, but the love of math eluded her. Questions like "Two men get on identical trains moving in opposite directions ... explain." You had to be a total computer geek to even figure out what the question was. And worse yet, Ms. Gretchen gave the worst homework of any teacher in the school. Stuff like, "for tomorrow's assignment I want you to list all the numbers. Please write legibly. This will count for ninety percent of your grade."

At least it felt that way.

It was an unfortunate time and place for her to be staring out the window, daydreaming, when two things happened at once. Ms Gretchen — noticing Candy was daydreaming — called on her to answer a question, and at the same instant a black car stopped on the street outside. She could not see the faces, but she knew they were watching her.

"Candy?" Ms. Gretchen repeated, "Are you with us today?" Candy's eyes were locked on that car. "Candy!" The driver's window rolled down a couple inches and a lens poked out. She could sense the person inside the car focusing on her. Then her vision was blocked by Ms. Gretchen. "Miss Tennison, I suggest you spend the rest of this period in the Principal's office." Candy sensed frustration from the car, and said nothing as she collected her books and bag and left the room.

It was only second period, on the first day of school. The Principal's office was empty except for the secretary and one student.

"Amy?" Candy was amazed. Amy was traditionally the "Good Citizen" award winner. "What are you doing here?"

"I punched Andy Bent in the face," she said without emotion. Candy took a breath and tried to catch a hint of Amy's feelings. She was feeling nothing.

There was a beep, the receptionist picked up a phone, then set it down. "Amy, you may go in." Amy stood and went in without looking at Candy.

Amy knew Ms. Springsteen, the Principal's Assistant, from last year when she helped out with the Spring program. Candy couldn't pronounce the name of the production; it had a strange Greek name. It was something the drama teacher had written. Candy played the part of a singing flower. A giant singing flower. She sang a song about the rain, and dogs, and children who came by and picked her friends. The audience laughed, but Candy found the entire play to be somewhat disturbing.

"I'm surprised to see you in here, Candy," Ms Springsteen said, she seemed sincere.

Candy was embarrassed. "I was staring out the window, not paying attention. You know math teachers, they just don't have a sense of humor."

Ms Springsteen grinned. Candy could tell it was genuine. And somewhere deep inside she could also detect a bit of dislike for Ms Gretchen the math teacher. And something else, something far away. Something sad. She couldn't put her finger on it. It made her want to walk over there and give the Principal's Assistant a hug. Maybe it was because she did a good job every day and didn't get any recognition for it. Or maybe it was because kids were kind of afraid of her because she worked in the Principal's office. Or maybe it was because she was … alone.

Alone? Candy wasn't sure where that thought came from. But in a flash – the kind of flash brains work in, where whole volumes of knowledge flash into your head before you even know it's there — she knew that Ms. Springsteen lived alone, had no special person in her life, and didn't like it.

Beyond the closed door of the Principal's office came a cry of agony. Then the door flew open and Amy came running out. Her eyes were red wet slits and her face was stretched like faces get when you've been crying. She tore right through the office and out into the corridor, the Principal, Ms Covad, came out right on her tail. "Amy, wait!" Ms. Springsteen hurried from her desk and followed them into the hall..

Candy hurried to the doorway. Amy had stopped down the hall to the left by the drinking fountain. Ms Covad and Ms Springsteen were standing with her, their hands on her shoulders. They were talking quietly, gently. They cared about her. There was a lot of emotion coming from Amy. She was angry, and afraid, and confused, and … lost. Candy was confused by it. Why would Amy

31

be acting that way? What had happened to her?

The school door to Candy's right clicked quietly shut. She looked over and saw a man and a woman, wearing dark sunglasses, dressed in business suits. They weren't going anywhere, just standing inside the door, staring at her. They were surprised. They had not expected her to be right there when they walked in.

Ms Covad noticed them immediately and hurried over, "May I help you?" she said.

Although she could not see their eyes, she was sure they were looking at her. They both held up identification. No badges that Candy could see, but little pictures and something which looked like an official seal, "We'd like a couple minutes of your time if you could spare it."

"Certainly," Ms Covad said. Candy stepped back as Ms Covad showed the two strangers into her office. The woman turned her head a bit as she walked by Candy, glancing at her.

"Candy," Candy jumped, it was Ms. Springsteen. "You might as well just go hang out in the library until your next class. I don't think there's any disciplinary action required here." She patted Candy on the back.

"Thanks." Candy hurried into the hall. Amy was already gone. She half expected to hear those polished black shoes clicking on the floor behind her, refusing to let her out of their sight. She could feel nothing from the man, an almost unnatural emptiness, as if he were trying very hard not to feel anything. But from the woman she had picked up a hint of … curiosity. And maybe a hint of fear.

Candy stopped at the water fountain. She had a sudden case of cotton-mouth. The water was cold, the stainless steel fountain whined and vibrated. Should she talk to her mom and dad about these people? She wanted to. She wanted to talk to *someone* about it.

Carl. She could talk to him. He would know what to do. Or not to do. It was strange; the thought of talking to her mom and dad about it was almost as scary as thinking about the people in the black cars. It didn't make sense. Nothing was making sense today. If this was what it felt like to be grown up, she wasn't sure she wanted it. Put her back in grade-school, when her biggest worry was who to play with at recess. Let her have that back and she'd be happy.

Chapter Three

Candy was on her hands and knees, gasping for breath, sweat running down her face, dripping from the tip of her nose onto the gym's hardwood floor. Her knees hurt from falling. Someone screamed and then a red playground ball hit her in the ribs. "Ouch!" she rolled away from it, clutching at the pain where the ball struck.

"You're *out* Tennison!" Wilma mocked from the other side of the line.

Candy was starting to sit up – eager to get out-of-bounds and rest her wounds – when Amy flew over her like a hawk diving toward its prey, rage burning in her eyes almost as bright as the red ball in her hands. She brought the ball back and let loose with a rocket. Wilma saw it coming but couldn't get out of the way in time. The ball made a loud *smack* sound as it hit her square in the face and bounced all the way back to Amy. Wilma went down flat on her back.

A whistle blew. "That's enough!" the teacher yelled. "Both of you are out!" Amy's face went from anger to surprise. Wilma's face was hidden beneath her hands. The idea of the game was simply to throw the ball to the other side and try to get the opposing player to drop it. But since Wilma had entered the game it had turned into Bruiser Ball.

A couple girls were standing over Wilma. Candy couldn't see through them. But she heard Janae say "she's bleeding."

Amy extended a hand and helped Candy to her feet. "You didn't need to do that," Candy offered. But secretly she was totally thrilled. She doubted any of Wilma's friends would back her up like that.

"Yes I did," Amy said, "let her get away with something like that, and next time she'll try something worse. Next thing you know she'll have grade-school kids buying her cigarettes," they laughed. It was nice to hear Amy laugh. Amy had said little of anything since the incident in the Principal's office that morning.

Candy glanced at the clock; just fifteen minutes until school was out. The whistle blew again, "wrap it up," the teacher said, the girls all headed for the locker room.

When the final bell rang, someone floating high above the Middle School would think it was a fire alarm from the way the small insect-like dots flooded out of the building, scurrying off in every direction, no apparent order to any of it.

Mostly the seventh graders, Candy thought. Last year she was one of those scurrying ants. But not this year. Eighth grade. She walked out casually, gracefully. Her

35

and Amy striding up the sidewalk and turning down the street toward Jan's house.

Within minutes the phone was ringing at Jan Slaughterback's house. This was the teen hangout. Candy and Amy came here directly after school before doing anything else. Amy didn't seem that excited about it today though. "She has cheesecake," Candy had teased. Amy grinned but didn't show her usual Cheesecake Euphoria. Jan was on the phone talking to someone about Andy Bent's bloody nose, a gift from Amy.

Tami Seltzer was already talking as she came through the front door, which was a little strange since no one was with her.

"Amy!" Tami squealed, "Oh my gawd that shot on Wilma was incredible, you were like a cannon or something, I just couldn't believe it. Is it true about Andy Bent? I didn't see it of course but I heard about it from Joyce Fouts during fourth period. I guess he was supposed to be in fifth period English but he wasn't there. Did he have to go home?"

Tami didn't just stand and talk. She wandered the room at the same time. She dropped her bag onto a chair, then danced over to the computer desk. Within minutes she was clicking her way to a chat room. She had always been the cutting edge member of the group. The first one to get her ears pierced, then the first to get them pierced *again* after everyone else started getting their first piercings. And the first one to show up wearing a nose-ring, although it turned out to be fake. Her mother wouldn't let her pierce her nose. Last year Tami turned into a Chat Room junkie. She spent several hours every day answering E-mail and hitting the Chats. There were over a hundred names on her buddy list. She had more friends online than she had at school. Probably because the online people knew her as 'Tiffany,' a seventeen year old blonde, six feet tall, who did teen modeling in Seattle.

"Being online is the next best thing to being a movie star," she said, "you can be anything you want and no one will ever know the truth." As she clicked her way toward the rooms she was also flipping through a magazine, looking at the ads. "Hey Candy, do you have a scanner?"

"You mean like for the computer?"

"Yeah."

"No. I think Jan's dad does, back in his den."

"Goodie," she said, still flipping pages. "They want a picture, so I'm thinking of ... *this one!*" She tapped excitedly on a picture of a teen model lounging on a beach in Mexico.

It was fun watching Tami work the Chats. She was very animated as she sat there. Moving her arms around, talking (of course), giving the thumbs up when something good happened, or frowning and dropping her chin into her hand if it was something bad. Candy could easily picture Tami on the weekends, sitting in a dark room, the only light coming from the computer. Tapping away at the keys; laughing at something someone wrote, raging when they said something bad.

Jan was a lot like Tami, except her weakness was the phone. From the minute she walked in the door, until her mother came home and yelled at her to hang up, she was on the phone, reviewing her day, talking about tomorrow, and anything else anyone wanted to talk about. Candy wondered how long it would be before Jan's mother got a third phone line in the house.

And then there was Amy; staring at the window. She had been up and down throughout the day. Right now she seemed down. Hiding whatever had been eating at her today.

With everyone occupied, Candy felt like a piece of furniture, just taking up space in the room, waiting for someone to come sit on her.

She pulled a photo album from the shelf under the coffee table and stretched out on the floor, flipping pages without interest. Jan when she was in fifth grade, Jan when she started kindergarten, Jan as a toddler at the beach, Jan with that weird cheese-goo all over her just seconds after being born.

Jan's parents looked so much younger in the earlier pictures. At least her mother. Candy had not seen Jan's father in a while. He left four years ago. Candy never heard the "scoop," other than the divorce stuff. Jan's house was the hangout because Jan's mother had a new boyfriend, and she usually had dinner with him after work. She wouldn't be home until after six. It gave "the girls" some serious chat time. Jan didn't like her mother's boyfriend, but she liked having the free time, so it was a tradeoff.

Jan came sauntering into the living room, the cordless phone pressed firmly to her ear as if she were digging out earwax with it. "Could you hold on a sec, there's another call," she pulled the phone away from her ear, hit the receiver, switched ears. "Hello? Oh HI!" Quick spin and back toward the kitchen. "Yes, she's here. Yes … no, didn't break it but he bled all over the place! It was great!" Her voice faded as she vanished into the kitchen again. Candy looked up to see Amy's reaction. She didn't say anything, but she wasn't staring out the window anymore; she was watching the back of Jan's head as it disappeared back into the kitchen.

"She should watch what she says on that phone," Tami said. Candy was surprised Tami even noticed Jan had been in the room. "Freebeezobo, this guy I know in Florida, says anybody can get a list of cordless phone frequencies. Anyone with a police scanner can listen to her call." Tami's eyes kind of glittered when she stared into a computer screen. It made her look a little crazy. "Freddy Blitzer lives just two houses away, he could be listening to everything she's saying right now. Listening to everything we're doing."

"That's great Tami," Candy said, she was still flipping pages in the photo album. She was curious about the way Jan's parents looked in those early pictures. She wasn't sure, but she didn't think her parents looked *that* much younger in their photo albums. Some people just age faster than others she guessed.

She couldn't ask Amy. Amy didn't have parents. Well, none that she knew of anyway. She lived with her Uncle Emmett in a little house a few blocks away. Again, Candy didn't know the scoop. Never heard the word divorce, or deceased, or adopted, or any of those words which usually explained why your parents weren't around. Amy's Uncle was not the nicest person in the world. Candy rarely went over there. He always seemed angry about something, and never too stable on his feet. He was bald with a weirdly discolored scalp, like he had a rash over part of it. His eyes were always kind of wet and runny and a little red. They looked like bad glass eyes, the kind you would find at a costume shop on Halloween. Every time she looked at him she expected him to start chasing her with a meat cleaver; like someone out of a horror movie.

Amy's gaze had wandered back to the window. Candy closed her eyes, relaxed, and let her mind creep toward Amy; sneaking into her like cold air around the cracks of an old window; the way she did when she was trying to feel someone else's feelings. Like she was sensing temperature, or color. It was hard to describe. But there it was. Some of the anger was still there, but there was something else beneath it; something strong. Fear. Fear to go home. Fear of her Uncle. There was almost no sign of the blinding rage which had been in her earlier. It had faded like old paint.

But when Candy thought about Amy going home to that little house and that angry man, it made her ache, as if it was her own life she was thinking of.

"You want to have dinner at my place tonight?" she asked. Amy looked up as if she had heard the words but was not quite listening. Candy felt confusion coming from her. Like being in the middle of a raging fire, thankful that someone had just thrown a bucket of water over you, but knowing it wouldn't last long.

"Sure," she said. "I have to stop by my house first though, pick up a couple things and let my Uncle know. Maybe I can find something in the garden. And..." she hesitated, "there's something I want to show you."

Candy had not seen the garden since last Spring when Amy first started working on it. The tiny back yard had been overgrown grass and wild shrubs. "Definitely. I need to see the garden before it's too late ... seasonally I mean."

The garden was important to Amy, it was one of the few things she did outside of school. Thinking about it made Candy sad.

Every summer the Tennisons went on a three week vacation, usually a driving marathon to places like Mount Rushmore, the Grand Canyon, Disneyland, Western Canada, or Alaska. Long, boring hours in the car, but there were always great moments and wonderful memories. That is, up until last summer when for whatever reason Dad didn't get a vacation. Candy had been bothered by that a lot.

But here was Amy; someone who had never had a vacation at all. Maybe she had never even been out of the state. Her Uncle had some sort of job which made him angry all the time, and when he got home he poured himself drink after drink and just made himself depressed. Last Spring Candy had talked to her Mom about letting Amy come with them on vacation, and it almost looked like it would happen, until their vacation got cancelled ... right around the time mom and dad turned paranoid.

"So," she said to Amy, deciding it was time to ask, "what was it Andy Bent did to get punched in the nose?"

Amy grinned. "He tapped me on the shoulder."

"What?"

"I know it doesn't sound like much. But he had been doing it over and over and I kept asking him to stop. Problem is ... that last time I think he really wanted something."

Candy grinned. The image of Andy reaching up and tapping Amy, just to ask an innocent question, and getting flattened. It was too much. She burst out laughing. Amy started laughing too. Candy rolled back onto the carpet, holding her stomach, laughing so hard her eyes started to water. It wasn't really that funny, but because they were laughing about it, it seemed even *funnier*. Like she was laughing at herself for laughing at something stupid.

The noise was enough to pull Tami away from the computer. "What?" she asked the two as they rolled back and forth. "What is it? What's so funny?" Watching them laugh made her chuckle. "Tell me-ee," she laughed. Amy rolled onto her back, tried to open her mouth to talk, but burst out again, and the face she made caused Tami to start laughing right along with them. "Tell me!" And like Candy she started laughing at herself for laughing about nothing. The three of them were like victims of a contagious infection with no cure; it would just have to run it's course.

Eventually Jan came in from the kitchen to see what the noise was. "What's so funny?" she asked.

Candy's stomach was started to hurt from laughing so hard. She rolled over and pointed at Amy, she took a deep breath. "You know why she punched Andy?"

Jan's eyes got big as if she had just opened a Christmas present. Here she was on the phone, talking about The Punch, and like a good reporter she was about to get a live scoop. "Do tell," she said.

"Because he …" Candy paused, and stopped laughing. It really wasn't that funny, and Jan would think it was downright stupid, "… because he called her a *chick*." Of course that wasn't really funny either, but Jan was a feminist, so she would agree that a punch was in order. Candy wasn't totally clear on what it meant to be a feminist, but she did know that it meant being mean to boys.

"I don't get it," Jan said, "what's so funny about that."

Candy's face was serious now, she wiped the smile away. "Nothing really," she said, "it just struck me as funny." Jan shook her head, pressed the phone back up to her ear and disappeared into the kitchen, deep in conversation. When she was gone the other three girls looked at each other, then started laughing again.

It was several minutes before the laughter finally faded away; all three girls flat on the floor, staring at the ceiling, trying to breathe normally. Finally Candy said, "We should get going. If I'm late Mom will think the Immigration Service picked me up."

Amy looked surprised, "You're an illegal alien?"

Candy grinned, "No, but she's been acting weird lately, that's just the sort of stupid thing she'd be worried about. You'll see."

"You're lucky," Amy said, "I'd trade my Uncle for a pair of whacked out parents any day."

Candy didn't say anything, she just looked at her friend and felt sad. Next summer, she thought, things will be normal again and we'll take a vacation and Amy can feel what it's like to be part of a family.

It was the first time in Candy's life she appreciated how special her family was. She remembered a campground in Eastern Wyoming a couple years ago, with a wide shallow creek and tall trees. Her and Carl had dammed up parts of the creek, forcing it to change course in some spots, and spill over their rock dam in others. Dad had let her build the campfire because she was the best at starting a fire with twigs and dead pine needles. Later, on a hike up a steep trail, Carl had slipped and almost fallen down an embankment. Dad screamed, rushed to him and caught him with one hand, then lifted him from the slope and swung him back onto the trail. It was one of those moments which was terrifying when it happened, but exciting to look back on later.

A couple days later – near Mount Rushmore – they had camped during a lightning storm. The wind was blowing so hard it pulled up three of the tent's seven stakes. Candy had been terrified, huddling near her parent's sleeping bag, but Carl had relaxed in the corner with his flashlight and a book. It had been her defining moment for Carl; the brave brother.

Over the summer – during one of their walks through the neighborhood – he had confessed he was terrified that entire night and could not remember a single word of what he read. "Mom and Dad were busy comforting you," he said, "I wanted to be strong so they wouldn't have to worry about me. But a couple times I was afraid I would wet my pants. I had to prop the flashlight on my pillow so no one would see how bad I was shaking." Maybe he thought he was admitting to being a coward, but Candy thought him even braver after that. Because isn't that what bravery is? Acting calm when you're really terrified? That's what Dad had said. Brave people are the ones who feel fear, but stand up to it. The ones who have no fear to begin with aren't brave, he said, they're crazy.

Chapter Four

"It's still summer!" Norman whined when he finally met up with Carl and James. They had been waiting more than fifteen minutes when Norman came lumbering out of the school.

Norman Botacelli was a tall round kid with greasy black hair and a pimple problem which had once hidden under his hair but was now spreading to his cheeks, chin, and nose.

The plan had been to hit James' house for a rematch of the Video Game Titans. Carl had totally spanked both of them yesterday afternoon. But Norman was having second thoughts. "We should be cruising the mall."

"We cruised the Mall half the summer," James complained.

Norman snapped his fingers. "It's a summer thing," he pointed to the sky. The chilly morning was long forgotten. It was a bright, warm summer day. "We'll have all Winter to hibernate." He looked to Carl for support.

"Technically," Carl said, "The Mall is indoors too. But ... whatever you want, I don't care." In Washington State there were only two seasons as far as high school kids were concerned: Summer and Winter. When Carl was little he called the seasons *sunny* and *rainy*. The rainy season was the long one. It would rain for a long, long time; then it was Christmas. Then rain for a long, long time again; then it was Summer. It was very simple. But then people taught him about years, and months, and days, and hours, minutes, seconds. They taught him how to make time totally drag, and how to get bored. They gave him boring things to do while counting those minutes and seconds: take out the garbage; clean the bedroom; mow the lawn; do the dishes; fold the clothes. There was so much to do. It made him wonder who had been doing all this stuff before him and Candy were born.

"Alright man," James said, "I don't care what we do, okay? We don't have to go over to my place. I just thought that's what we agreed to do this morning?"

"Well that was this morning," Norman said, "it was cold and I figured it would be fun. But look at this!" he motioned to the sky. "It's still summer. We need to cruise!"

"Okay," James said, "let's cruise."

The mall was just a few blocks from the High School, so every day after school boys and girls could be seen cruising the long continuous canyon of stores. Rarely did they buy anything. The Mall was not a shopping center, it was a social center. A place to vent; a hangout. Teenagers walked up and down the mall's length, looking for people they knew from school. This was what Norman meant when he said they needed to *cruise*.

Carl was a tall, good-looking fifteen-year-old who attracted a lot of attention from the girls at school. Unfortunately for them — and much to the shock of his friends – his head wasn't into girls yet. He didn't go to dances, didn't hang out with girls from his classes; he preferred to just hang out with his friends, or read. Carl was a voracious reader. Textbooks, novels, magazines, comics, whatever he could get his hands on. So two places at the Mall attracted him like magnets. The bookstore, and *The Comic Hut* which also had a lot of used paperbacks. So it was lucky for Carl that *The Comic Hut* was just a few feet away when Norman began babbling incoherently about nothing at all.

"No really," Norman rambled, "the stereo was fine before I borrowed your CD … it was rockin' the tunes bay-bee …"

James and Carl looked at each other as if to say "what's he talking about?" Then they both saw the group of girls on a collision course; four of them. Dressed brightly and fashionably in shorts and summer dresses; lots of tanned skin. They were all talking at the same time. One of them was eyeing Norman, it was Kelley, his blonde dreamgirl. Light blue eyes, long straight blonde hair which cascaded far below her waist. She was wearing a dark green tee shirt and Beachnaw jeans which were tight around the waist but baggy around the legs. Carl had to admit the girl was hot. And from the look on Norman's face, a tornado could rip the roof off and he wouldn't notice it.

Carl did not look forward to getting caught in a conversation with those girls. So he jumped ship. "I'm going to check out the books," he said, pointing to the Comic Hut. The idea of trying to talk to that group made him very nervous. He would stumble and stutter and end up saying something stupid; another embarrassing moment to haunt him the rest of the school year.

"I'll hold his leash," James said, nodding toward Norman who was still rambling on about stereos and CDs.

The Comic Hut was the tenth store to occupy this space in the fifteen years the Mall had been here. Four had been clothing stores, two sold greeting cards, two toy stores, a discount miscellaneous item store and then over a year ago The Comic Hut settled here. It seemed to be doing well. The cashier was sitting behind a row of glass cases running the length of the store, behind her were taller cases filled with rare collectible comics, books, and trading cards. The rest of the store was filled with bookshelves. Rows and rows of shelves lined with books and comics, some new, but most were used.

Carl headed right for the A's in fantasy. He loved the Lorena Alicia fantasy books. They were long; the shortest was over eight hundred pages, which meant they were expensive to buy new.

For a moment he just stood at the head of the row. He loved looking at shelves loaded with books. It would be great to freeze time, park on the floor, and dig into these books without any interruption.

A wall of conversation formed in the Mall outside The Comic Hut. Norman, James, and the girls had made contact. He couldn't understand their words, only a blending of sounds, like waves at the beach. He could sense it's energy; like fusion inside the Sun; it could go on forever. The emergency exit at the back of the store suddenly caught his attention. That would be the only way out if he wanted to avoid the painful social scene on the Mall. A grey metal door with a bright red bar across the center. "Alarm will sound," written in bright bold letters.

He kneeled down at the first row. Greeting him like an early Christmas were dozens of Lorena Alicia books; it was better than Christmas. He was thumbing across the titles when he felt the presence. It came at him the way sounds do when you first wake up. When your eyes are still shut, and you think you're still dreaming, but the sounds of the world creep into your head as if someone just flipped a switch.

It didn't startle him even though he knew the *presence* was following him. There were two people, male and female, and they were feeling a little fear, and a little … what was it? Awe? Why would someone direct a feeling of awe toward him?

For a second the feeling went away, but then out of the corner of his eye he saw a black polished shoe. He didn't look up, "what do you want?" he asked.

"Carl Tennison?" the woman asked. She had been standing beside the man, just out of Carl's vision. When she spoke the man stepped back and she stepped up. Carl stood and faced her. She was about six inches shorter than him. She took a step forward, too close, like she expected him to back away. He didn't.

"Yes?" he said. "You want something?" His voice stayed calm even though his heart was racing and he felt his hands trembling. He could sense her fear rising; it calmed him a little.

"We just want to talk," she said. She tried to keep her eyes locked on his, but a couple times her eyes flickered away, over his head or off to his right. She was afraid to look him in the eye.

"Then talk," he said, and kneeled back down to thumb across the books. He picked one, a thick one, over a thousand pages. It was book seven in the Macatia series, his favorite series, and the only one he didn't have. It had only been out in paperback a couple months, he was surprised to find a used copy. A discovery like this would have been the highlight of his day, if not for the two people standing over him. Typical that adults would find a way to take a wonderful moment and make it uncomfortable.

"My name is Tara Blake, this is David Curtis," she said, pointing to the man behind her. Carl glanced up at her, she was wearing a black knee-high skirt with black pantyhose and a black jacket with a white blouse and black tie. All very official. She was wearing a pleasant smelling perfume. "We're with the FBI." He raised an eyebrow at that, looked at them both again, then returned to his book. "We've been assigned to keep an eye on your father."

Carl stood, "What do you want with my father?" He could not hide the irritation in his voice now. It increased the fear he felt coming from the agents.

"Your father is mixed up with some bad people," she said, "it's not his fault. But when the hammer falls, it's going to fall on him as well as them." She paused, looking in his eyes. The man was still fearful, but the woman was feeling confident. "You can help him Carl. They're about to make a move and if we know about it in advance we can stop them. If you help us we promise that no charges will be brought against your father."

Carl did not trust either of these two. But they had one big advantage over him. They knew what they were up to. He could only guess. If he refused to help them they might do something to keep him from warning his father. "My dad has been acting strange lately," he said, trying to sound worried. "What can I do?"

The woman held back a relieved grin. "Just tell us if he plans to leave town suddenly … and when." She reached into her jacket and handed Carl a small business card. It was plain white, with just her name and phone number. "It would help us out a lot, and help get your life back to normal."

"Sure." He said, looking at the card. The number was not local. "Where is this?"

"You can call collect," she said. She turned as if she was going to walk away, then turned back and said, "Carl, I know you have no reason to trust us. I have no idea what your father may or may not have said to explain his recent behavior, and for all I know you're going to run home and tell him all about this," she paused, took a deep breath and let it out slowly, "but you have no reason *not* to trust us …"

"How do I know you are who you say you are?"

She hesitated, looking him in the eye. "I think you

52

can … sense … that we're not lying to you Carl."

That startled him. They knew about it … that he could sense their feelings. Without realizing he was even doing it he reached out for her feelings. There was a tiny bit of fear, a little worry, some excitement, and … what … honesty? Was she really telling the truth? She seemed to be, although there was something back there he could not pick up. As if she was telling the truth, but not the truth he was hearing.

Like the time he was wrestling with Norman, trying to judge his moves by his feelings. "This isn't going to hurt, is it?" he had asked. "No," Norman had said. And Carl had trusted him. What he didn't realize was that Norman's version of "hurt" was not the same as Carl's. It *did* hurt, but Norman had not lied because he honestly believed it wouldn't. Something like that was happening here between him and these two FBI agents. But he was not about to challenge them, because if they thought they lost their hold on him they might decide to pepper-spray him right here and haul him off to a holding cell somewhere.

"Yes," he said quietly, "I believe you. Now if you'll let me look at books I would be grateful."

The agents left without another word. The woman was feeling a sense of relief like you feel when you leave the dentist. The man was feeling relief as if a gang had been about to beat him senseless then let him go instead. Why is he so afraid of me? Carl wondered.

He thumbed through the books, but had lost his interest in them for the moment. Deep inside he needed to talk to Candy. Not about this, but about anything. Just to know she was nearby and alright and not feeling as uneasy and … afraid … as he was.

He was having one of those "moments." The lights seemed too bright and his ears picked up every little sound. Customers mumbling, the lights buzzing, the sound of air moving through the heating system, the drone of voices in the mall. Norman's faraway voice and the chattering giggle of those girls. Bad things always seemed to make the world more real; and good things made you feel like you were living in a dream. It seemed backwards from the way it should be. And in the middle of it: Carl Tennison, age fifteen. Not a child — although most of the time he still felt like one — and not a man, although those FBI agents were pushing him in that direction faster than he wanted. It was a confusing feeling. Frightening, uncertain. This was the sort of thing parents were for; to go home and talk to. "Dad, this is how I'm feeling, what is this about? Why am I feeling this way? Is this normal? What am I supposed to do?"

But was this something he dared talk to his Dad about? Was his Dad really mixed up in something illegal? He didn't think so. But these people were official. If they weren't really police then they were something else; something worse. They had not showed him any identification. No FBI badges with their pictures. FBI agents on television always flashed a picture I.D. and a badge. Not these two. Maybe they were Mafia, or CIA, or something else. Something so secret that even the X-files hadn't done an episode about them.

54

Why put this all on me, he thought, I'm not even old enough to drive! It wasn't a fun day anymore, not a good day to hang out at the Mall with his friends. He just wanted to go home.

James and Norman were both laughing along with the girls. The sound was like a barrier; prison bars preventing him from leaving the store. He felt trapped, cornered, no way out and no desire to join the laughter. It felt uncomfortable. It felt wrong. There was probably another way out besides that emergency exit; an employee entrance or a shipping entrance. A door into a service corridor. He calmly walked over to the cashier, trying not to attract the attention from his friends outside.

He pointed to his friends outside, "Is there … another way out of here?"

The cashier, a young woman, smiled and pointed him toward a curtain behind the counter … and freedom.

Willoughby Tennison wiped the sweat from his hands as he stepped into The Spar Café. Sitting alone at a table in the far corner he saw Gheorge. They exchanged polite waves as Willoughby made his way to the table.

"What's the emergency?" Willoughby asked, even though he pretty much knew.

"We're pulling everyone out," Gheorge said.

"What?" Willoughby had expected his family to get pulled, but not everyone.

"The entire Olympia operation has been corrupted," Gheorge said, "it might be limited scope, but they don't want to take any chances, so they're pulling everybody out."

A waitress came over. Willoughby asked for coffee, Gheorge just wanted water.

"When?" Willoughby asked.

"Tomorrow night," Gheorge said. He was watching Willoughby's reaction carefully.

"That's too soon," Willoughby said.

"Why?"

"We need time to get things together."

"Don't you get it Tennison? This isn't some planned meeting or vacation trip. This is all-out evacuation. They're watching you. They're watching your family. They're all over the schools. You start *getting things together* and they'll know something is up. They'll drop on you before you have a chance to get your guard up." He frowned at Willoughby, expecting an argument, but Willoughby said nothing. "You and your family will be at the rendezvous point at exactly eleven o'clock tomorrow night or there'll be questions asked which you might not want to answer. There's no time to waste. Take what shouldn't be found, and leave the rest."

Willoughby took a deep breath and stared out the window at the people walking down the street. Twenty years he had lived here. He met Arlia at this very place.

They both knew this moment would come; they had feared it since the day Carl was born. Last spring the black cars had started showing up, and they it was close. Now here it was. They had been discovered, and procedure demanded they leave; but Willoughby did not want to leave, and neither did Arlia.

This was their home; they would not leave it. But he wasn't about to say anything now. It wouldn't do any good. The time for words was over; the time for action was at hand.

"Very well," he said, "we'll be there," but he could not tell from the man's face whether he believed it or not. Willoughby knew the family was being watched. He had already been approached by The Watchers and given an offer. An offer he never intended to take, but one he had hoped would buy him time. Now his own people were putting the pressure on. Time was up. The idea of running did not scare him half as much as the idea of trying to convince the kids why they needed to run … and what they were running from.

Chapter Five

Once upon a time, Amy's street had been clean and beautiful, lined with trees, white picket fences surrounding sturdy wood frame homes, station-wagons in the driveways and kids playing baseball in the street. Over the years the trees had either been blown down by storms or cut down by the city utilities department so they wouldn't get in the way of the electricity and telephone lines. The picket fences had fallen apart and not been replaced. The homes had been sold to people who lived in other cities and rented to people who didn't care that the plumbing was rusty and the paint was chipping away.

Children sometimes played on the sidewalks, but most of the time they were in fenced backyards away from the eyes of strange neighbors; rarely did anyone play in the street. There was a busy avenue just a block away, so on the weekends the teenagers would spill over into this area, bringing with them noise, vandalism, and attempted burglaries.

Amy lived in a small three-bedroom wood-frame house in the middle of this neighborhood. The white paint was chipping off the siding, revealing aging grey wood underneath. Weeds covered the yard which was overdue for mowing. That was Amy's job; one among many.

The front door was warped. After turning the key in the lock and twisting the doorknob, Amy had to bump her shoulder hard against it to get it open. The living room was dark and smelled like sweat, socks, and beer. The TV was on but the sound was turned down. Amy hurried Candy through the darkness into a narrow hallway which led to her bedroom. She practically threw Candy into the bedroom and quickly closed the door behind them, but not before Candy heard the Uncle mumbling in the kitchen. Something heavy fell on the floor with a dull thud.

Candy felt a lot of feelings surging within the walls of this house. Amy was feeling scared, and embarrassed, and angry, all at once. But the most confusing feelings were the ones coming from the kitchen. Candy could not even begin to put them together. It was confusing, frightening, and quite unpredictable. And beneath it all, supporting it like the foundation of a house, was something dark. Something buried so deep that Amy's Uncle spent a lot of energy trying to keep it out of his thoughts. It made Candy shiver, she had to pull away from his mind to stop it.

Amy rifled through a drawer, stuffed a couple things into her backpack, then grabbed Candy's hand. "Out the back," she said. She led her back into the hall, paused in front of the door to the kitchen, then hurried through. Uncle Emmett was kneeling over a spill on the floor.

"Where you been?" he shouted with a bit of a slur.

"Got held up at school," she said, then nodded her head toward Candy, "you remember Candy?"

Moist red eyes considered Candy for a moment, then turned to Amy. "Where you think you're going?"

"I'm going to show Candy the back yard."

"Don't take long ... dinner soon."

"I'm going to have dinner at Candy's," Amy said, Candy felt the tension rise, as if she expected a harsh reaction. From the Uncle she felt anger and disappointment, and then suddenly ... nothing. As if a wave had washed the feelings away. He grunted something and turned his attention back to the cleanup.

The old screen door creaked as they hurried into the back yard, it slammed hard behind them. Uncle Emmett yelled something which they could not make out. Amy paused for a moment, making sure he wasn't going to follow them.

The backyard was small and fenced in, thirty feet across and the same distance deep. But where the front yard looked neglected, the backyard looked like a garden. The lawn was rich green and well mowed. Along the left fence were flowering plants of brilliant colors; yellow, purple, orange, and red. Along the right fence were well-trimmed hedges, looking almost artificial in their perfection. Near the back was a garden.

"This is where I live," Amy said. Candy could feel

her tension wash away. The garden was near the end of its seasonal cycle. There were still some cucumbers growing, and some carrots, and bean plants were growing along stakes near the fence which separated the back yard from the alley. There was also a little carport where Amy's Uncle kept his truck; it was dirty and rusty and looked like it couldn't be depended upon to even get out of the alley. Between the carport and the garden Amy had planted a row of Sunflowers; standing tall like a living fence. Happy yellow faces looking down on the vegetables.

"Watch the alley," Amy said, "this is what I wanted to show you. It shouldn't be long." They continued to poke around the garden, but after just a few minutes there was a quiet motor and the sound of gravel crunching under tires. A black car drove slowly by, dark windows hiding the driver and passenger. Candy felt the color drain from her face.

"They've been coming by for a couple weeks now," Amy whispered, "I think they're waiting to bust my Uncle for something."

"Did you tell him?" Candy asked in a tiny voice.

"No," Amy said without emotion, "he deserves whatever he gets." She leaned down and poked through the broad leaves and thick vines of the cucumber plants. Her hand vanished into the green jungle then emerged with a long thick cucumber, it's green skin dotted with what looked like tiny porcupine quills. "Do you like cucumbers?"

"Love them. My dad would live off them if he could."

Amy picked more, Candy was surprised how many cucumbers were still growing this late in the season. Eventually both girls were holding several cucumbers each. "I'm not sure there are any good carrots," Amy said. She fingered the base of a couple stalks, pulled a couple up but only found one good one. "Uncle Emmett tends to come out and eat the carrots," she said, "he tries to blame it on wild rabbits."

No wild rabbits, Candy thought, but you've got people in black cars driving around keeping an eye on you. Just like they're keeping an eye on me.

Chapter Six

Arlia Tennison was mashing potatoes when Willoughby came through the door. She could tell by the look in his eyes that something was wrong. "What did Gheorge want?" she asked, even though she was sure she already knew.

"Mandatory evacuation," he said, "tomorrow night."

Arlia dropped the potato masher into the pan, her head dropped, her shoulders sagged. "Oh no," she said.

Willoughby put his arm around her, she buried her face in his shoulder. "It's alright," he said, "we're not going to do it."

"We knew this moment would come eventually," she said.

"Have you changed your mind?" he asked. "Do you want to go with them?"

"The kids ..." she began.

"Get their lives turned upside down regardless of

what we do," he said.

The back door opened suddenly, they both jumped; startled. Carl walked in, breathing heavy from running. He didn't look particularly happy.

"Hey honey," Arlia said.

"Hi," Carl said. He glanced quickly at his parents then headed for the living room.

"Dinner's almost ready," she said.

"Okay," he was gone.

"How can we do it without being seen?" she asked.

"We have our plan. We stick to it. If we're lucky they'll all trip over themselves trying to stop us. We have to be ready though, we might be forced to move sooner than we want."

She nodded. Hugged him again.

"Where's Candy?" he asked.

"She's not home yet," Arlia said, "I'm a little worried. I called Jan's and she said they left over half an hour ago."

"They?"

"Amy is coming with her."

"I don't like it," he said, "those people snooping around … maybe they went to Amy's. I'll give her Uncle a call." He patted her on the shoulder and hurried toward the living room.

Several minutes later, as Arlia was setting food on the table, Candy and Amy stumbled through the back door trying to balance their book bags and handfuls of cucumbers.

"You took your own sweet time," she said, trying

not to sound worried. "Where have you been?"

"I was over at Jan's house, then stopped at Amy's to get some cucumbers."

Willoughby shot into the room as if someone had been screaming for help. "There you are young lady," his voice louder than it needed to be, "you've had us worried sick!"

Candy felt a little anger stirring inside her. They can chew on her for being a little late and she has to explain herself, but they can worry her and Carl all summer and not say a thing about it?

"I'm not later than usual on a school day," she said. "I always stop at Jan's."

Carl stepped into the kitchen, like a knight on a white horse. "Same as she always does," he echoed, "is there something going on we should know about?"

He said it casually, as if just tossing it out there. But it weighed heavy. It was every worry and every late night walk they had all summer. Everything compressed down to one innocent sentence. Candy's heart was beating wildly in her chest. She could feel the color rising in her cheeks. Carl looked calm but his face paled a little, his cheeks got rosy. Arlia stared at her husband. Willoughby looked from one child to the other.

"No," he said in a calm voice, "we were just worried." He had defused the moment without offering them even a hint of what had been bothering them.

Amy's emotions had not changed at all. She had no clue anything was going on with this family, other than being the Average American Family. She was feeling …

what … warm and fuzzy? That was it. She was feeling comfortable here in the Tennison kitchen. Like a kid on the Brady Bunch, just one of the family.

Candy felt bad. This was the type of moment she took for granted. Mom and Dad here every day when she got home from school, and every morning when she woke up. Amy had nothing like this. This was a vacation for her.

"Cucumbers from Amy's garden," Candy said.

"Cucumbers," Willoughby said, his eyebrows rising. "My favorite fruit. Green condensed sunshine right there." He took them all and piled them next to the sink. He had a paring knife and saltshaker in his hands before Candy could protest.

Amy leaned toward Candy's ear, "they're vegetables, not fruit."

Willoughby heard, "It's a fruit," he said, "look it up. Any seed-bearing flesh is fruit. In fact, most *vegetables* are either roots, or the body of the plant itself. Like eating leaves." He already had one cucumber peeled. He sliced it lengthwise and salted it liberally. "This," he said gleefully, "is fruit." He took a bite, closed his eyes and chewed slowly. "Nothing like this …" he whispered. Arlia hit him on the shoulder.

"There's enough for everyone," she said. She motioned everyone toward the table where fried chicken, mashed potatoes, green beans, toasted sourdough, and now cucumbers, waited for them.

Amy devoured the food as if she had not eaten for days. Willoughby silently feasted on three entire cucumbers before bothering to put anything else on his plate. By that time there were only two pieces of chicken left, the rest were slaughtered remains on Amy's plate.

"How was first day?" Carl asked Candy.

"Same old," she said, "you?"

"Nothing special," he said.

Arlia cut in, "That's not what I heard," she said, "Jimmy Morlana's mother told me you had a little excitement there today."

"Oh?" he said, "which excitement was that?"

"Something about someone trying to break into lockers or something? And you chased them out of the school?"

"Oh," he said, "yeah," he looked at Candy. "A suit in a black car." Candy's head popped up when he said that. Her look said everything he needed to know. She had been seeing them too. He glanced at his parents and saw what he expected from them; they were looking at each other with genuine concern.

"Are there any more potatoes?" Amy asked, licking the last from her fork. "Those are really good. You're a really good cook Missus Tennison."

Arlia smiled, "Well thank you," she said, "I just don't get complements like that anymore. The secret is using chicken broth instead of milk." She took the potato bowl over to the stove and scraped the last of the mashed potatoes from the pan. Amy was reaching for them before the bowl was back on the table. "So Amy ... if I may ask ... what happened to your parents?"

Candy shot her mother a look. This was not the

67

time or place for that sort of thing. She looked toward her dad for support, but he was looking at Amy with genuine interest, as if he had been the one who asked.

Amy didn't skip a beat, "I don't know," she said softly, scraping the last of the potatoes onto her plate, "I don't really remember them. I know they were there once, but Uncle Emmett just says they had to go away," Arlia and Willoughby exchanged concerned looks, then Willoughby started peeling another cucumber. "That's all he'll say about it," she said, "and there's no one else I can ask … so … " she played with a forkful of potato, "… I just try not to think about it too much."

Candy could feel a barrier in Amy's mood. There was more to the parent story than that, but she wouldn't tell it. Or couldn't tell it.

"Well," Willoughby said as he bit into another cucumber, "you inherited a definite talent for growing sun fruit."

After dinner they gathered in the living room. Carl had a sitcom turned on, Arlia was sitting on the sofa pretending to watch and read a book at the same time. Candy and Amy were sitting on the floor near the front door, Candy had grabbed a photo album from the shelf in the hallway.

When Willoughby came into the room he looked out the corner of the closed curtains before sitting down on the sofa. Candy and Carl looked at each other briefly.

"Where's this?" Amy asked about a picture in the photo album.

"Wyoming," Candy said, "this campground was

really cool. It floods during the winter from rain falling in the hills."

Amy flipped the pages back to the beginning of the album. "Is this little baby Carl?" she teased. Carl looked at her but didn't respond.

"Yep," Candy said, then stopped. There was baby Carl with that cheese goo on his head, and there was Mom looking tired and pale, but otherwise almost exactly as she looked right now. And a picture of dad holding baby Carl … also the perfect image of the man she was looking at right now.

"You guys don't age at all," Amy said, pointing to the pictures. Candy watched as her mother and father said nothing, but looked at each other very intensely. Arlia looked at Willoughby almost pleadingly, as if she wanted to say something which he would not let her say.

"Our families don't look old until much later," Arlia said, "Candy's grandparents looked very young well into their seventies."

"Really?" Amy flipped quickly through more pages, "are there any pictures of them in here?"

"No," Arlia said, "they died some time ago. They lived in Europe so we didn't see them very much."

"I don't remember ever seeing them at all," Candy said.

"Me either," Carl said.

"You were both very young the last time you saw them," Arlia said, "I wouldn't expect you'd remember them."

"Aunts, Uncles?" Amy asked.

"None," Arlia said, "Willoughby and I were both only children," she smiled, "I guess maybe that's one of the things which drew us together. We're both Only Brats."

Amy was feeling sad. It was a strong feeling, but Candy could not tell where it was coming from. Maybe it was because she was an Only Child too. Or maybe she was sad about having to go home. Candy looked away and tried not to feel it too strongly. She saw Carl looking at Amy too, as if he were feeling the same things. Then she noticed her parents, both looking intently at Amy.

"Are you going to spend the night tonight Amy?" Arlia asked. Candy was shocked. It was odd for Mom to be asking something like that on a school night.

There was a sliver of hope, and fear in Amy. "I'd love to," she said, "but I'm not sure my Uncle would go for it on a school night."

"I'll call him," Arlia said, "I'm sure it will be alright."

Amy's face lit up, "That would be terrific!" she said. She looked at Candy, they both made big faces and grinned widely.

Arlia was in the kitchen for some time. She never raised her voice, but she talked longer than she needed to and a couple times Candy detected the "angry but in control" voice which her mother often used on them. Eventually she hung up and came back into the living room, smiling, "it's done. I'm sure Candy has a clean nightgown somewhere you can use."

The girls both squealed in joy and raced into Candy's room, where for the rest of the night it felt more like a weekend sleepover than a school night.

It was shortly after midnight when Willoughby quietly closed the bedroom door. "Everyone is asleep," he said.

Arlia was sitting up in bed, nervously tapping her fingers against the back of her hand. "So what are we going to do?"

"Well, Gheorge is expecting us tomorrow night, so we'll have to move before then."

"Those others are around all the time."

"I know, they're outside right now."

"How do we get away from them?"

"We have options there," Willoughby sat down next to Arlia, took her hands in his, "I think we can use them to help us, and they won't even know they're doing it."

"And the kids?" she asked.

"Well, we're going to have to talk to them, obviously."

"They're not going to believe it."

"Not right away," Willoughby agreed, "but eventually they will. Especially if things start to go wrong. Is the Displacer charged?"

"Yes. I've got it in my purse."

"Well ... I guess it's like a rollercoaster now. We take the ride and hope the car doesn't come off the tracks."

Chapter Seven

Candy shot up out of bed. It was still dark, the clock-radio said five thirty. Someone had just whispered her name.

"It's me," Carl whispered.

"What's going on?" she whispered back. There was a glow outside from the streetlight, it was enough for her to see the outline of Carl standing over her. She was tucked into her sleeping bag on the floor next to her bed, where Amy was nestled under a thick purple comforter, breathing slowly and evenly; asleep.

"They're here," Carl said. She didn't need to ask who *they* were. "They're talking to Dad."

"Where?"

"In the living room," he motioned for her to follow him, one finger over his lips, telling her to be quiet. They crawled to the door and he opened it a sliver. They couldn't see the living room from here, but they could hear voices. Too quiet to make out what was being said.

"Where's Mom?" she asked.

"I don't know. Maybe she's still asleep." He stepped carefully out the door and tip-toed toward the living room, Candy was right behind him. They stopped before the end of the hallway, still hidden by shadows. A few feet ahead of them a single light from the living room illuminated the end of the hallway. It would be too dangerous to venture that far.

"We can get you out before they even know you're gone," a woman's voice said. Carl recognized it from the Mall. It was Tara Blake, the woman who had talked to him. Maybe she had been telling the truth; maybe Dad was mixed up in something bad. He looked back at Candy, she was there, motionless, a look of concern on her face. She could hear it.

"Okay," Willoughby said, "But you need to back off first, so they'll think you're losing interest. The less you're watching the less they'll be watching."

"Agreed."

"And it needs to be in the evening. That gives us time to do it before anyone notices anything has happened."

"We can do that."

Carl could sense a third person out there, not saying anything. Probably the man, David Curtis. The woman was feeling a sense of near joy, the man was still afraid.

"Okay," Willoughby said, "I'll need about a week to …"

"Not a week," the woman interrupted. "Mister Tennison, I'm very sorry but we cannot pull our people back for a full week. I want to cooperate with you in any way I can, but I can assure you that my superiors will not agree to a week. We need to move on this as quickly as possible."

"How quickly?"

"Tomorrow."

"That's too soon."

"Actually it's almost too late. Our project leader is going to be in town this afternoon with instructions that we move one way or the other. If there's anything you need to take care of, we can do that for you after the relocation. Nothing will be lost."

There was silence for a moment, the two agents were suspicious. Carl started to worry they knew he was here; he expected to see their heads poke around the corner.

"Alright," Willoughby said. "But we need to make it look smooth. We can't do it here. Give me a location and we'll be there at six o'clock."

"Why so late?"

"My kids get out of school, they need to go through their normal routines. Nothing should look sudden or rushed. We'll have dinner, then go out in the car, nothing unusual there, we could be going to a movie. In fact … can we do it at a theater?"

"Certainly," the agent said. She had a feeling of satisfaction, again, the difficult puzzle coming together.

Carl heard Willoughby stand, he waved Candy back. She turned quickly but silently and headed back toward her room. Just before the door Carl tapped her on the shoulder and motioned her to his room. Once inside he looked back to make sure they weren't seen, then quietly closed the door.

"What's that about?" Candy whispered, fear rising in her voice, "where are they taking us?"

"They cornered me at the mall today," Carl said, "told me Dad was in some sort of trouble and if I helped them they'd make sure nothing happened to him."

"What sort of trouble?"

"I don't know. They said he was in business with someone they were watching."

"So where are they taking us?"

"I don't know. Maybe a government safehouse or something."

Candy was quiet for a moment, then said, "Carl … I'm scared."

"Me too … but look … whatever it is, they have to tell us about it tonight don't they? I mean … there's no way to just brush this off."

"I guess so."

"It'll be alright Candy."

"I know. I just … I don't want to leave my friends," her voice cracked, a tear ran down her cheek. "I know it sounds stupid, but … Amy needs me. I can't just leave her with her Uncle. He's horrible!"

"It might not be that bad. Maybe just a couple days, then the cops will do whatever it is they're going to do and then we'll be back."

"You think so?"

He paused, "I have no idea. But I hope so."

They stood in the dark for several minutes. Finally Candy said, "I can't go to school today and just act like everything's normal. What am I supposed to do?"

"I don't feel like it either. But we need to do it." He patted her on the shoulder, trying to comfort her. She dropped her head onto his shoulder and hugged him. "Go back to bed. Look at it this way … one way or another, by tonight we'll know exactly what's been going on."

She nodded and slipped back to her room, but she did not sleep. She lay there on the floor, half covered by her sleeping bag, staring at the ceiling and listening to Amy's breathing. Life had a base to it. Something which you always expected to be there. Something which made it feel safe. But right now she felt it slipping away. It was as if this house which she had grown up in, with all its memories and all her possessions, was turning to dust right in front of her, and there was nothing she could do about it. This time tomorrow all this would seem to be gone and she would be clinging to her parents for support again. A little girl, afraid and small, hiding from the scary shadows.

At least I have parents to cling to, she thought, sad again for Amy. For a friend in need whom she would have to abandon, at least for a little while.

She laid there, staring at the ceiling, images flashing through her mind. Her parents looking out the windows, the black car at the bus stop, the black car …

… the black car at Amy's house! Oh no. Her heart raced. They were about to run from someone, from something, but Amy might be in the same danger. The same people were watching her.

Thinking about it made her heart ache. Her friend, alone. A miserable life and no one to turn to. The sky outside the window was starting to glow with the sunrise. On a normal morning it would seem beautiful, but right now it seemed threatening; dangerous. She didn't want it to happen. She wanted the sun to go back down so the night could hide them in shadows forever. Hide them from everything.

At seven o'clock her alarm went off. She sat up quickly and dressed. Amy dragged herself up slowly, taking a moment to wipe the sleep from her eyes and let them adjust to the light. "Wow," she said, "you really wake up perky."

"I woke up a little while ago," Candy said, "I was just laying there enjoying the moment."

"Whatever."

Candy had heard her parents moving around for a while. She had been tempted to go out and talk to them.

"Coffee," Amy said, "I never smell coffee in the morning. I've walked right into a family TV show haven't I?" She grinned. Candy could sense the happiness Amy was feeling. She tried to share it, to drain a little of it from Amy and feel it herself. She wanted to very much. Anything to ease the tightness in her chest and the shaking in her hands. She wanted to cry. But she needed to keep a happy face on for Amy.

"I think half dad's blood is caffeine," Candy said.

Carl was already at the table eating a bowl of cereal. He didn't look up when Candy and Amy came into the room. Willoughby was at the table drinking a cup of coffee, Arlia was microwaving frozen breakfast muffins.

"What would you like girls?"

"I don't usually eat breakfast," Amy said.

"Oh," Arlia said, "you've got to eat breakfast. It's the most important meal of the day. At least have some cereal." She glanced at Willoughby, then said, "girls, dad is going to pick you up after school today. Would you like to join us for dinner again tonight Amy?"

Candy's eyes darted to Carl who looked up quickly from his cereal.

"Sure!" Amy squealed. Then she frowned slightly, "but I'm not sure my Uncle will go for it after spending the night and all."

"I'll talk to him about it," Arlia said, "I'm sure it'll be fine with him."

Amy turned to Candy and made big eyes. "Terrific!" she said.

"Why are you picking us up from school?" Candy asked.

"We just thought it would be nice to do something together tonight," Arlia said, "and thought it would be nice to include Amy."

"Not getting any complaints from me," Amy said.

Carl hurried out to catch the bus. An hour later Candy and Amy stepped out the door. Candy expected to see black cars lining the street, but there were none. Not one. Nothing at the bus stop either. Everything seemed overly quiet. Even Wilma Jenkins was quiet. At school there were no black cars. During Math, Candy stared out the window almost the entire period and never saw even one black car drive by. For a while she was able to convince herself that last night had been nothing more than a dream.

Then everything started to go wrong.

Chapter Eight

It was Jessica Sharpe's thirty-eighth birthday. She was reminded by the flowers and card she found on her desk. They were from her mother in Florida. There was a nice poem inside the card, and scribbled birthday wishes in her mother's handwriting. She didn't bother to read it. "Happy Birthday to me," she said as she moved the flowers to an empty computer table in front of the window. The tall office window faced west. It was in a building in downtown Denver, Colorado. In the distance the hills rose quickly, but this morning everything was hidden by the clouds. It was the kind of view which made visitors from the East think the Great Plains and the Rocky Mountains met in Denver.

Jessica had long dark hair which hung down to the middle of her back. She was tall, almost six feet, but still enjoyed wearing heels. Today she was in a black business suit and skirt with black pantyhose and thick-heeled, open-toed shoes. Her mother would call it a younger woman's outfit. She caught her reflection in the window and felt ridiculous for a moment.

"I'm not that old," she said to the reflection. But she sure felt it this morning. Just two years away from forty. The big Four Oh. And what to show for it? A government job? Doing things no one could ever know about? Looking for people who might not even exist?

But yes, she thought, they do exist. I know. I've seen them. They took something from me, and I want it back.

Ten years married to her job; chasing the memory of a dark night, and three strange people who could not possibly have been human. Ten years of research and dead ends. But now it was close. She could feel it. Something big was just around the corner.

She sat at her desk with her back to the window. It was the only way she could avoid staring outside, getting lost in daydreams.

The office and a couple assistant's offices were part of the National Security Agency, but as far as the public knew these were offices of a private advertising firm. It even had an ad in the Yellow Pages. It was such a well maintained cover for agents that there were some real advertising people employed here. They had developed one of the commercials shown during the last Superbowl; a popular thirty-second piece about penguins and dolphins rebuilding the world after an asteroid collision.

Jessica's *permanent* office was in the NSA building in Washington D.C. But for the last year she had been working at offices in Chicago, Seattle, and here in Denver.

These were considered "Special Assignment" offices and were much nicer than her little hole in D.C. Her regular office was half this size and had no window. She didn't miss it.

But she did miss her apartment in D.C. For a year she had lived in motels. Always moving from one to another. Even when she stayed in one city for more than a week she was required — for security reasons — to switch motels every four days. Why it couldn't be seven days, or ten days she had no idea. Someone with a lot of authority — or more likely a committee — had picked four days as the maximum time an agent should stay in one place. They probably took a lot of time and spent a lot of money to reach that decision.

She checked the clock, ten minutes before nine. At Nine o'clock she would need to be parked at the computer, the tiny camera on top glaring into her face so she could participate in the weekly conference call with the Project Leaders, most of them based out of Geneva, Switzerland. An odd location for a United States Federal Agency to be located.

Unfortunately, the clouds started to clear and she could see into the hills. A crystal clear view which extended for miles. She started daydreaming without realizing it, and the next time she looked at the clock it was five after nine.

"Oh no!" she yelled as she spun in her chair, facing the computer. The screen wouldn't come on fast enough and the computer seemed to boot up very slowly. Her online connection failed twice before she finally logged on. There were two full minutes of security checks and passwords before she was able to log into the conference call.

"Nice of you to join us," a man said. "It worries us when people are not here on time."

"I'm sorry," she said. Her screen was only displaying the chairman, a man in his fifties with thinning grey hair and solid, serious face, as if he had just stepped off Mount Rushmore.

"Status," the Chairman said.

Other people would stutter or act nervous after appearing late and suddenly being asked to give a report. But Jessica was good under pressure, that's why she had the job.

"Our field agents stepped up the operation on the Tennisons last Spring. Two weeks ago they made contact with Willoughby, and yesterday they made contact with the son. They say he was politely cooperative. Two of the agents were to attempt to make contact with the Tennisons last night or this morning. I don't have a report from them yet."

"Coverage?" A voice said. It was not the chairman. A smaller male voice, higher in pitch. One of the Project Leads. She thought she recognized it as Stan Woodwell. He was in Calgary.

"We have twelve in the area covering the Tennisons and people we suspect to be their contacts. Another twelve are coming in today, and we have coverage on exit points. I'll be heading to Seattle this afternoon and should be field co-ordinating in Olympia by this evening."

"Probability?" a woman said. Lynnea Halston. The last time Jessica had talked to her she was on assignment in Arthur, Nebraska. As dangerous and out of the way as an agent could get.

"We assume the Tennisons have been here for a very long time, so they probably won't scare easily. We don't know what their escape plan is."

"For all we know," Lynnea said, "they can just de-materialize from their house and we won't know for days."

"Not likely," Jessica said, "the Phillips – in Orlando – ran, and gave away a rendezvous point. I would think if they had a way of disappearing from under our noses they would use it."

"Agreed," the chairman said. "Continue, and we'll expect a report tomorrow morning."

"Very good," she said.

"On time," he stressed.

"Yes sir," she said, "again, I apologize for my tardiness." She was glad they had not mentioned Hennesey. He had vanished into thin air right under their noses and had not been seen since. Previous lost agents had popped up in strange locations ... like Australia. But not Hennesey ... not yet.

But if left the question ... if these people could do things like that ... why did they bother to run? It made no sense.

She wasted no time signing out of the computer. This was her last day in the Denver office. Regardless of what happened over the next few days in Olympia, she would not be returning here anytime soon. She pressed the "reassignment" icon and the computer began forwarding files to her computer in Washington D.C. and deleting them from this one. She opened her briefcase and stuffed it with her files from the desk, including some really nice pens she had picked up here. She wasn't really supposed to take the pens, but they wrote very smooth and didn't leak; she couldn't avoid the temptation.

She pressed the intercom button, opening the line to the secretary. "What time is my flight out?" she asked.

"Noon, Miss Sharpe."

"Thank you," Jessica said. Miss indeed. What does it take to get people to say Ms? Probably an official memo from a committee. Maybe a committee is working on it right now, she thought. Probably been working on it since the sixties, spending millions of dollars and travelling all over the world to do research on it. She wouldn't be surprised.

She stood in front of her window for almost a half hour, just gazing out at the view, and daydreaming. She appreciated a good view, and she would certainly miss this one.

At lunchtime Carl was sitting alone at one of the round cafeteria tables, picking away at the hot pizza lunch. He had been distracted and daydreaming all morning.

"Hey Carl," James Morlana said as he slid his tray onto the table, "you've been a zoner all morning. What's going on?"

"Nothing."

"How about that vid rematch after school?"

85

"Can't. Dad's picking me up after school."

"What for?"

"I don't know. Him and Mom want us to do some family thing tonight."

James was quiet for a moment, then said, "That's kind of weird isn't it? Right in the middle of the week?"

"Nothing's weird lately with my parents."

James chewed slowly on a rubbery piece of pizza. "What'dya mean?"

"Just stuff. Parent's going through a mid-life crisis or something."

James asked something after that, but Carl wasn't paying attention. His mind was on the two FBI agents, and his dad, and wondering what was really going to happen after school.

Chapter Nine

It was seventh period when things starting to go wrong. Amy wasn't in class. This was the only one they shared, PE. She was tempted to run from class looking for her, but she wouldn't get far before getting an invitation to the Principal's office for the rest of the period. Fortunately it was a lecture day – better health through exercise and proper eating – so she didn't have to really *do* anything. She sat with her binder open, absently scribbling in it, pretending to take notes. When the period ended she hurried to the office. Out the front doors she could see her dad waiting with the station wagon.

"Yes?" the secretary said.

"Amy Nottingham was supposed to go home with me today? But she didn't show up for seventh period?"

"Yes," the secretary said, "her Uncle picked her up right after lunch."

"Oh," Candy's stomach knotted up. This couldn't be good. She stood there for a moment, feeling weird.

Kind of afraid and alone. Like she was running through a black room with no idea how to get out and no one there to help her.

"Is there anything else I can do for you?" the secretary asked.

"Uh … no … no, I'm fine. Thank you," she turned toward the doors, not even noticing when they opened.

"Where's Amy?" Willoughby asked.

"Her Uncle took her home after lunch," she said, "wasn't Mom going to call him?"

Willoughby's brow lowered in a frown, "she did," he said, "I thought everything was fixed up. We'll see when we get home."

"So what are we doing tonight?" Candy asked.

Willoughby didn't answer right away. They were a couple blocks from the school when he said, "there's something your mother and I need to talk to you and Carl about." He glanced at her, noticed the worried look on her face. "It's nothing bad … really … it's just … some changes. Some things are going to be a little different. We'll explain it all when we get home."

When they stepped through the front door, Carl was on the sofa. Arlia was right next to him, holding his hand. He was staring at the window as if he couldn't see anything. His face was pale.

"He's alright," she said to Willoughby, "where's Amy?"

"Her Uncle took her," Willoughby said. Arlia's lips formed a surprised "oh."

Candy felt very uncomfortable looking at Carl. He

88

looked like someone had died. He wouldn't look at her. She needed him to look at her so she would feel like everything was okay. So that whatever was about to happen to them, she would know they would make it through it together. But he just sat there, staring.

"Sit down," her father told her. "We've already had a little talk with Carl, but there are things both of you need to know." Carl still wasn't looking at her. "First of all ... there's some things about you we need to tell you."

Oh no, she thought, they're going to tell me they're not my real parents. They're going to say I'm adopted, or they kidnapped me from a mall when I was a baby, or something weird like that. Maybe I have a disease?

The room started to bend and turn. She was dizzy. Her father put his hand on her shoulder; it made the room stop moving.

"You can sense what other people are feeling, can't you?" he asked.

"Yes," she said.

"And you noticed in the photo album last night that your mother and I have not aged in the fifteen years since Carl was born?"

"Yes."

"And you've never seen any of your relatives."

"No."

There was a long pause, as if he was searching for the right word. He looked at Arlia, then stared for a moment at Carl. "Do you believe in life on other planets?"

It was a weird question. Probably the last one she would have expected. "I don't know," she said, "I guess so."

"I do," he said, "you want to know why?"

She nodded weakly, "yes."

"Because I was born on another planet."

She grinned. But dad didn't grin back, and neither did mom. And Carl ... Carl finally looked at her. His eyes were still kind of blank, but there was pleading in them, like he was asking her for something.

"What?" she asked her dad.

"I was born on another planet. So was your mother."

There was no answer to something like that. Nothing that she could think of. There were a couple possibilities. One, her dad was teasing, which didn't seem likely at the moment. Two, her dad really thought he was from another planet, which would make him a complete nutcase, and three, he was telling the truth; which was impossible.

"We don't expect you to believe it right now," Arlia said, "we just need you to trust us and go along with things. You'll learn soon enough."

"You can't sense what I'm feeling, can you?" Willoughby asked.

She reached out to him, trying very hard to sense his feelings. But there was nothing there. It wasn't as if he had no feelings, it was more like there wasn't a person there to feel. If she closed her eyes she couldn't tell he was in the room.

"You can't sense your mother either," he said, "or Carl. Because we're all alike. We're all from the same place. You kids were born here, but you're not *from* here."

Candy could not absorb it. She didn't want to absorb it. Suddenly her parent's heads turned at the same time toward the street. Then back at her. "What do you feel out there right now?" Willoughby asked.

She reached outside. It wasn't hard to pick up. "The people in the black car," she said, "four of them. Two men, two women. The women are concerned, one of the men is afraid, the other doesn't seem to care about anything. Why are they going to take us away?"

Willoughby's eyes grew wide. "How did you know .... well ... they're from the government, Candy. They know who we are. They want us to go with them to a *facility* in New Mexico where we'll be safe and where they can study us and learn from us."

"Safe from what?"

"When something like this happens," Arlia said, "when the government finds out who we are and where we're living, we're supposed to go ... back home."

"To our own world," Candy said flatly.

"Yes."

"And of course we can't go, right? Because we don't have a spaceship in the garage, or a transporter or whatever we need to beam up. Right?"

Her parents frowned. "Candy," Arlia said, "we know it's hard, and we don't expect you to believe. But believe us when we say we're not going with those people."

"But Carl and I heard Dad talking to them this morning. He said we're going with them tonight."

"I just said that to distract them long enough for us to get away."

"Get away where!" she screamed, "this is crazy! This doesn't make any sense!" Tears were pouring from her eyes now, dripping from her cheeks. These were her parents, they were supposed to make everything okay. They were supposed to make her feel safe. This was like one of those movies where everyone you know turns out to be an alien or an agent or a demon. Anyone but who you expect them to be.

Carl rose from the sofa and walked slowly toward her. He put his arms around her. "Let's just get through tonight," he said, "everything will be okay." He guided her toward the door to the garage. He was trying to be the brave big brother, but she could feel him shaking.

Her parents were hauling bags out to the car, Carl helped her into the back seat then settled in beside her. She heard her mother say, "what about Amy? We can't just leave her with that man."

"We'll drive by there and see what the situation is," Willoughby said.

"Do we have time?"

"Probably not."

They sat in the garage for several minutes. Willoughby had backed the car in and closed the door when they had come back from the school. Now he sat, hands on the wheel, staring at the closed door.

They're crazy, she thought, both my parents are crazy. They've totally snapped and now they're running from the police. We're going to get arrested, or shot. Me and Carl will end up with Foster Parents. I won't have a family anymore. I'll be worse off than Amy.

Something clicked in her head. She could feel the people in the car driving by. That's what Dad was doing. Feeling for them and waiting for them to drive by. They weren't parking right in front of the house tonight, because that was the agreement; they said they would back off. But that didn't stop them from driving around the block, just to keep an eye on everyone. She could sense them as the car passed by and then went around the corner. As soon as it turned, Willoughby started the car, opened the garage door, and pulled out, turning quickly in the opposite direction. He paused just long enough to make sure the garage door was going back down.

Willoughby had always been a safe driver. But not now. He gunned it as they hit the street. Tires squealed and Candy and Carl were sucked back in their seats as the car raced away from the house. Four blocks away he turned right; out of sight of anyone watching the house. He slowed down then, but not much. "We're going to stop by Amy's," he said. "Even if you think your mother and I are crazy, you have to admit she's better off with us than with her Uncle."

Candy could not honestly say that. But she would welcome having Amy here. Another shoulder to cry on. Maybe they would end up in the same Foster Home.

When they turned the corner onto Amy's street Willoughby stopped the car suddenly. Two blocks away police cars filled the street in front of Amy's house. Including three of the black cars.

"Oh no …" Arlia said. She fumbled in her purse and pulled out her electronic organizer. In an already crazy situation it seemed like a crazy thing to do. What was she planning on doing with it? Adding up last month's grocery slips? Maybe she was going to look up the phone number of a good UFO expert.

"Too late," Willoughby said. He looked back and put the car in reverse. At that instant Candy could feel Amy.

"Wait!" she said. Amy wasn't in the house, she was close, hiding. Candy reached out quickly and desperately. Somewhere up on the left, across the street from her house, in the hedges.

"There's no time," Willoughby said, "I'm sorry Candy."

She didn't wait to argue. She had the door open and was out before the car moved again.

"Candy!" Arlia yelled, but she was already sprinting for the sidewalk. She was holding Amy in her mind, trying to pinpoint her position. She didn't want to draw attention to herself by screaming Amy's name.

Two police cars had the street blocked at the corner, Amy was hiding somewhere close to them. Candy stopped behind a group of onlookers being kept back by a police line. Looking back and forth through the bodies she caught a glimpse, Amy in some bushes maybe thirty feet away.

Candy slid to the left until she was away from the people, near the edge of someone's yard. If Amy turned she would see her. Suddenly someone grabbed her arm and turned her around.

Candy!" it was Carl, "Let's go!"

"She's right there, Carl! Can you see her?"

Carl leaned forward, squinting in the direction of the bushes, he saw her. He glanced around quickly, then started walking toward her. He didn't get far before one of the police stopped him.

"Can't go through here son."

"But …"

"Do you live around here?"

"No, but my sister got past you, she's over in those bushes I just want to get her out."

The officer looked in the direction Carl was pointing and saw the figure in the bushes. He nodded and let Carl through. Amy didn't see him until he was almost right on top of her. She jumped and started to run, then recognized him and stopped.

"What are they doing?" she asked. Her voice was shaky; Carl could sense the terror in her. It was so intense he could feel himself starting to shake just from sensing it.

"I don't know," he said, "but we're getting you out of here. Take my hand, stay close, and *run!*" They sprinted away from the bushes. The police officer who let him in was standing with his back to them. Carl was sure the officer would think it suspicious that they were running like this. He made eye contact with Candy and motioned her to start back toward the car. She didn't move, something had startled her.

Candy noticed the change immediately. From the direction of the house, probably from the people in the black cars, came a surge of feeling. Recognition. Alert.

Panic. They saw Carl and Amy, they knew who they both were. There was yelling from near Amy's house, and pointing.

"Stop them!" someone yelled at Carl. The officer who had let him pass turned, noticed who they were pointing at, and moved in front of Carl. Carl tried to run past, but the officer grabbed him by the back of his shirt and jerked him violently back. Carl came off his feet and fell backward onto the ground.

Whatever fear had been gripping Candy was temporarily ripped away when she saw her brother thrown to the ground. She launched herself at the officer, leaping onto his back. He was braced for an assault by Carl, not for a rocket hurling itself at him from behind. The force threw him forward, onto the ground. Carl rolled back onto his feet, grabbed Amy and ran. Candy leaped from the officer's back and sprinted behind them. No one in the crowd tried to stop them, they all just stared as if they were watching something unfold on television.

Willoughby had turned the car around, he was screaming at them to hurry. The three kids piled into the back. The tires were squealing before Carl had the door closed behind him.

"Are you kids alright?" Arlia asked. Candy and Amy were locked in a hug, both sobbing in fear, neither said anything.

"We're okay, Mom," Carl said. He was looking back. Two of the black cars were hopping the curb to get around the police cars which had the street blocked.

"Arlia ..." Willoughby said.

"I know," she said, "I'm ready."

They sped down several side streets, tires squealing, the kids being tossed from side to side in the back seat. Carl tried to fasten his seat belt, but finally gave up and hung onto the door handle.

"How many of the black cars were back there Carl?" Willoughby asked.

"Uh … I saw three I think … yes, three."

"And one at the house," Arlia said.

"We might need an extra battery," Willoughby said.

"We're fine."

In minutes they were out of the city limits, on a county road which would lead them to the freeway. Willoughby was still speeding like a maniac. The tires squealed around a corner, then Willoughby slammed the brakes and brought the car to a sudden halt. Blocking the road ahead, two shiny black cars, three men standing in front of them, pointing rifles.

Candy thought she was going to be sick. Carl was frozen. It was one thing to have crazy parents, another thing to have no parents at all, and even worse to be helpless in the back seat while police shoot at them.

"Okay," Arlia said. She tapped desperately at the keypad on her pocket organizer. It was too much for Candy to see. Mom and Dad gone nuts. Willoughby pressed the gas pedal to the floor, the car leaped forward, racing toward the people with the guns. Candy looked at Carl, his eyes were locked on the people up ahead. Candy felt warm tears filling her eyes, she wanted to scream. Dad was going to ram those cars, or those people were going

97

to shoot him! Arlia held up her pocket organizer, pointing it at the cars like a TV remote control. She pressed a button.

FLASH! A bright flash, like a bomb exploding, but without a boom. Candy closed her eyes but it didn't stop bright orange and red spots from appearing before her. For a second she was afraid they had been shot at. Is this what it feels like to get shot? She wondered. Am I dead? No, she thought, not dead. I feel fine, just blinded.

She wasn't completely blinded. She could see well enough to tell the windshield had not been broken. And she could see the road. It was …

… the road was …

The road was empty. No black cars, no people with guns. No big black spot on the road where an explosion had been. There was nothing. It was as if the people and the cars had never been there.

Amy had her face buried in Candy's shoulder, but both Candy and Carl saw it. Mom pointed her organizer, there was a bright flash, and the cars went away. Their mouths dropped open, they stared at each other. A wonderful thing was spreading inside them. The idea that maybe their parents weren't crazy after all.

"It's alright," Arlia said, "they're not hurt. They've simply been … relocated."

Candy stared at the spot as they drove through it. She looked back as they passed it … still no one there. No sign of anything. No wet spot on the ground, or fragments of car, or anything. "To where?" she asked.

Arlia looked at her display, pressed a couple buttons. "Um ... Denmark, I think," she turned around and looked at Candy, "Are you starting to believe?" She held up the organizer, "Anyone on this planet have something like this? That you know of?"

Candy looked at Carl. His eyes were wide, he was shaking his head slowly. Amy looked up from Candy's shoulder. "What happened?" she asked. She looked behind them and saw the empty road, "where did they go?" All Candy or Carl could do was stare at her. They couldn't think of anything to say.

Arlia grinned at them, "Let's just get out of town," she said to Amy, "then we'll fill you in." She smiled at Willoughby; he returned it. They didn't speak, but they knew they had taken a big step. A very big step.

Chapter Ten

"Tara?" Jessica Sharpe stood in the street, next to her car. Around her were local police officers and on-lookers. Amy Nottingham's house was surrounded with yellow police tape; agents were removing things from the house, each one carefully wrapped in plastic to avoid contamination before they could be examined in a lab.

"Tara!" She had her cell-phone up to her ear, she had been talking to Tara Blake at the roadblock. The line had gone quiet. Not like Tara had hung up; but like she just wasn't there anymore.

"Not again," Jessica said. Then a computer voice came on the line. "The Web-cell customer you were talking to has moved out of the service area …"

What did we do wrong? She thought. We made contact, we were nonthreatening. Then it occurred to her. They probably pulled their guns. She had told them not to. No guns. No good will come of pointing guns at them. But Tim Anderson had been the lead agent in that group; he was raised on old cop shows. He was the kind of guy who would spend his evenings at home in front of a mirror pointing his gun at his reflection, saying things like "stop, or I'll shoot!" or "you talkin' to me?"

Two cars and eight people. Not dead, she knew that. But somewhere very far away. Hopefully not somewhere dangerous.

Just like Atlanta, she thought, two families, everything seemed to be going well. Then an agent started threatening them and the next thing she knew they were calling the D.C office from a village in Tanzania.

Well, the Tennisons had slipped away. So now it was not an easy task. She knew they were not going to cooperate … at the moment. Step one was finding out where they were going. The terrific thing about Western Washington State was the ease in tracking someone trying to get out. The Pacific Ocean to the West, no exit there. They won't try leaving on a boat, it would be a floating trap. North is the Canadian border, easy to place agents at the border crossings. East are the Cascade Mountains, a limited number of passes to get across, easy to place agents there. The biggest hole in security would be south, toward Oregon. And from Olympia that route was only two hours away.

Jessica motioned to an agent stepping out of the Nottingham house. He hurried over.

"Ms. Tennison?"

"Pretend you're trying to get away from me," she said. "What's the fastest route? Where would you go?"

He thought for a moment, he was a local agent,

based in Seattle. He knew the area well. "South," he said, "freeway all the way. Two hours from now I'm in Portland and my options open up."

"How's that any better than here?"

The agent paused, he looked a little embarrassed. "The vortex," he said. She looked at him but said nothing, he took that to mean she didn't understand, "The Oregon Vortex, a magnetic anomaly which occurs only two places in the world ..."

"I know what it is," she said, "How many agents do we currently have available?"

"Twenty four," he said with a raised eyebrow, she should know their number better than him.

"We just lost eight," she said, "I need border coverage and pass coverage but I want the emphasis on Oregon. Get their license plate number to the locals, I don't want them stopped, just tracked." She started to turn away, then turned back to him, "And I need the D.C. office alerted that they might be getting an overseas call from eight agents assigned to us here. We need them back as soon as possible." She slid into the back seat of her car, the driver tilted his head back, waiting for instructions. She had never been to the Portland office before, but she knew you could see the Cascades from there. Maybe the office had a nice view.

Tara was in the car, she had been talking on the phone to Ms Sharpe. There was a knot in the pit of her stomach, like something nasty wanted to come back up. She was trying to find a way to tell Jessica that Tim and

David were standing outside the car pointing rifles at the Tennison's station wagon, then a bright flash blinded her.

The phone went dead, she heard something bump the car, probably David falling over, blinded. She blinked rapidly trying to get her sight back. The sounds outside had changed.

Bright red, orange and white spots flashed every time she tried to focus on something. She covered her eyes, waiting for them to fade. After a moment she realized what the new sound was; rain. It was raining hard. Maybe a water main had been broken by the bright flash. The car door opened and three agents poured in. They were gasping.

"What was that?"

"What happened?"

"Where are we?"

That was a peculiar question, she thought. Water was running down the window, obscuring her view. She could see well enough now to see the digital display on her phone, it said *No Service.* That was odd. Then she saw something through the watery frame of the window. She rolled the window down, wind hit her face, cold rain stung her eyes, but she saw.

Windmills. One close, a few others in the distance. And fields. Broad endless fields. No sign of the paved road they had just been on.

"This isn't Olympia," she whispered. She felt awe, and respect for the Tennisons. To have the power to do something like this. And to be kind enough to do this rather than hurt them, which no doubt had been an option.

The Global Positioning System on her beeper was searching for a new satellite signal. It found it, then displayed her new position in latitude and longitude. She couldn't read latitude and longitude, so the numbers meant nothing to her. The car's GPS system included a Geographical interface and database, so in a matter of seconds it was telling them exactly where they were. It took a moment for the driver to comprehend what the display was telling him. "Denmark," he said, "we're in Denmark."

Tara looked back out the window at the windmills. "Awesome," she said. The others just looked at her.

In a small town a half hour south of Olympia, the Tennison's pulled into a coin operated car wash.

"Carl," Willoughby directed, "give it a rinse then run hot wax over it." He handed back a handful of quarters.

Carl stared at the pile of coins in his hand. We're on the run from the government and from aliens, but we're taking time out to wash the car? He slipped out the door without saying anything.

Candy knew that even though Carl was acting calm, he was as terrified as she was. And a sudden car-wash in the middle of a desperate getaway did not earn her parents any 'sanity' points.

Willoughby took something from under the seat and got out of the car. Arlia dug around in her purse, then turned to the girls and handed them a couple granola bars, "Are you two doing okay?" The girls were huddled together, as if they were one person. They took the bars, unwrapped them slowly, and chewed as if everything were happening in slow motion. "I don't know why they were taking your Uncle, Amy. Maybe they think you have something to do with us."

"Why do they want us so bad?" Candy asked. The shock of watching her mother make cars disappear was wearing off. Her brain was having trouble accepting it. And Amy was having an even tougher time. She had said very little since getting into the car in Olympia; she was shaking. Candy could feel her terror, an almost crippling fear, but Candy could not tell where the fear was aimed. Had something happened with her Uncle before the police arrived? Was she afraid of the people chasing them? Or was she afraid of Candy's parents? Come to think of it, Candy wasn't sure herself.

When Carl turned the hot wax onto the car it began to change color. He stopped.

"Keep going," Willoughby said, "it's supposed to do that." He opened the package from under the seat; it contained a screwdriver and two new license plates. He kneeled behind the car, away from where Carl was spraying, and placed the new plate over the old.

The car had been dark blue, but now it was changing to white.

"We should have monitored what you watched a little more," Willoughby said, "movies and TV make the idea of aliens believable, but at the same time make people who believe in them seem like crackpots."

Carl wanted to say something, but no words would come. Nothing which would make sense anyway. "I don't know dad ... I just ... I don't know." Water and hot wax sprayed over the windows. He saw the images of Candy and Amy in the back seat, Candy was talking to Mom but he had no idea what they were talking about.

"Twenty years ago," Arlia said, "we came here to learn and observe. At first we were single people. We were supposed to meet and marry Earth people, but as fate would have it, we ran into each other instead," she grinned, her eyes lost focus as she looked through the back window at the crouched image of Willoughby. "Talk about finding a needle in a haystack."

"So there are others," Candy said, "other than us?"

"Yes. A lot. I don't know how many though. They certainly didn't like your father and I getting together. It wasn't part of the plan, but they went along with it."

"Who are *they*? Do I know them?"

Arlia thought for a moment. "The Heaths," she said.

"The Heaths? The guy who makes me call him Uncle Walnord?" Candy started to giggle. She turned to Amy, "this guy's pants hang half down his butt ..." she burst into laughter, "... and he's an alien ..."

"We don't know who else is based in Olympia," Willoughby said, "we only know our contact group."

"So when do you meet them," Carl asked.

"Every other week, downtown at the Spar. We have

106

a little get together, exchange reports for transfer back home, have a couple cigars. Just some businessmen having a lunch for all anyone else knows."

Carl's doubt was not as deep as Candy's. Since the first moment his dad had claimed to be an alien a question had popped into Carl's mind.

"Dad ... a couple years ago, when we were on vacation, coming home from Mount Rushmore ... we stopped at a rest area in Wyoming."

"I remember," Willoughby said.

"You made us stay there until dark. Candy and I sat out watching shooting stars with Mom ... and ... for a while it got very quiet. And we didn't know where you were."

"I was meeting someone. That was the first time we were warned that we might be watched."

"I saw them leave," Carl said, "like a large shadow, rising over a ridge, staying kind of low to the ground. Didn't make a sound."

Willoughby's eyebrows raised. He grinned. He knew he had won his son into believing. Perhaps he had won him a long time ago.

"How does it work?" Candy asked. Arlia was holding up her pocket organizer.

"Well, it has many functions. Everything from just a normal calculator to ... to the Displacer."

Candy pointed to a garbage can across the parking lot, "can you make that disappear?"

"No," Arlia said.

"But Amy didn't see the cars …" Candy began.

"As soon as I turn it on it will give away my location. That's supposed to be a feature. It allows them to find us and … rescue us … if we ever get into trouble."

"Does it do other … alien things, other than make things disappear?"

Arlia paused, she looked down at the organizer, almost sad. "Yes," she said, "but none of that really matters anymore. It's best not to get into it."

The car was completely white, Carl was rinsing the hot wax as Willoughby fixed the new plate on the front of the car.

"So where are we going?" Carl asked.

"We don't have a definite plan," Willoughby said, "I guess the less predictable we are to ourselves, the less predictable we'll be to them. I figure we'll head south a ways, then maybe get on Highway 12 and cut over the pass. Then see what looks good tomorrow."

"What do you think they expect us to do?"

"What the government people think depends on what they know," Willoughby stood, stretching his back. The tension of the day was tightening the muscles from his neck all the way to his legs. The pain was starting to show in his face. "I don't think our people will be a problem for a couple days."

"I don't get it. Why are we running from our own people?"

"When they found out we were being watched,"

Arlia said, "they ordered us back to the Homeworld." She paused, looking far away. Remembering something. "That's the standard procedure. Get us away before there's any threat. I'm surprised they left us here as long as they did."

"So why don't we go?" Candy asked.

"We don't want to go," Arlia said. She grinned. "We like it here. We met here. We fell in love here. We made a life here. You kids were born here. This is our Home World now ... not that one."

The car doors opened, Willoughby climbed back into the driver's seat, Carl slid in next to Candy. "We're set," Willoughby said. "Been having a good talk?"

Arlia smiled, looked at the girls, "I think so," she said.

"Us too," he said, grinning at Carl.

Carl looked at Candy. "I believe them," he said.

Candy hesitated for just a second. Long enough to make her mother worry. "So do I," she said.

"I don't know what to believe," Amy said, "but I'd rather be with you guys than with my Uncle."

"Tell us about the Home World," Candy asked, "what's it called?"

Arlia and Willoughby exchanged glances. "It's hard to explain," Arlia said. "Our world doesn't have a name ... it has ... hmmmm ... I'm not even sure how to put it. It has a symbol. It has an ... idea." The kids said nothing. "Like the way you can sense people's feelings," she said. Candy glanced nervously at Amy. Amy didn't seem to understand. "On our world people don't communicate with speech. They communicate directly through thought. There's no language, just a direct transfer of ideas. We never developed that in you, but traces of it surfaced anyway."

"It's like talking about an apple," Willoughby added, "we wouldn't use the word apple. We wouldn't even think the word apple. We would think of the apple. We'd picture it, and transfer the picture to your thoughts. And not just the picture, but all our knowledge of the apple. It's flavor, it's texture, the fact that it grows on trees and gets brown and rots, and has seeds in the middle. All that in a single thought. It's much quicker."

"And much more accurate," Arlia said, "there's never a misunderstanding."

"Do you and dad do it?" Candy asked.

Arlia grinned. "No," she said. "That's one of the things we like about being here. Speech. It's slow sometimes, and it can be frustrating. But there just seems to be a lot of depth to it … a lot of feeling. It's romantic to piece things together like this."

"What's the Home World like?"

"I don't know what it's like anymore," she said. There was a note of sadness to her voice. "I haven't been there in twenty years. Even more time than that has passed since I last touched it's soil. And things were changing fast even back then. The sky isn't blue though, it's kind of lavender. And there are two suns, so we don't have a consistent day and night like they have here." She stared past them, out the window. Candy didn't ask more.

They drove in silence for almost an hour. When

Willoughby turned off the freeway and headed toward the mountains they stopped and ate dinner. The sun was starting down and some high clouds were passing over. Enough to hide the shadow which moved through the clouds, hovering near the restaurant. The shadow which followed them up the highway as they fled into the mountains.

Chapter Eleven

It was after dark. The tires hummed on the rough highway in chorus with the rumbling thunder of the engine. Candy and Amy were asleep, leaning against each other. Arlia had not spoken for some time, Carl assumed she was asleep as well. They were somewhere in the mountains; the music on the radio faded in and out. Carl stared out the window, occasionally lights would pass in the distance, sometimes near the road. Houses tucked away in the trees.

A couple times he nodded off, drifting into strange dreams. Dreams that he was at school, and the Principal was telling him his parents were crazy and had run off with Candy and he would probably never see them again. The school was dark and empty, no one there but him and the Principal. The entire world felt like that. It was not a good feeling, so when he woke, he tried to stay awake.

But being awake didn't feel much different than the dream. In some ways it was worse, because he couldn't wake up from it. Yesterday he had been a normal teenager, starting his second year of High School. Getting back together with some friends he hadn't seen too much over the summer. Planning on spending the school year reading, doing homework and playing video games. No reason to think anything weird was about to happen. Now he was a fugitive.

And something else. He wasn't really human, was he? Last summer he and Candy had talked about how weird it would be to find out they were adopted. This felt kind of like that. Like suddenly he wasn't the person he always thought he was.

"Dad?" he said quietly, careful not to wake the others.

"Yeah, Carl?"

"Who are the people in the black cars?"

"They're United States Government people. The National Security Agency."

"They told me they were from the FBI."

Willoughby looked at Carl through the rear-view mirror, "they talked to you?"

"Yeah, yesterday. They told me you were in some sort of trouble and they wanted me to tell them if you tried to leave town."

"Hmmm."

"What do they want with us?"

"They want us to move to New Mexico. Live somewhere down there where they can study us, and talk to us, and learn about our world. And keep an eye on us so we don't try to take over, or corrupt the country, or whatever

113

ugly thing they might suspect aliens of trying to do."

"Would it be so bad to live in New Mexico?"

"It could be. It's not a normal life. It's not the kind of life we want for you and Candy. It might be okay for your mother and me, but once you kids are grown you'd want to leave. And they probably wouldn't let you. We want to live on Earth, but we don't want it so bad that we would live in conditions like that. If it came down to an absolute choice between the two, we'd go home."

"Is home so bad?"

Willoughby didn't answer right away. Carl almost thought he hadn't heard him. "No," he said, "it's not that bad. It's just that ... well ... life here is simpler. There's more opportunity. It's kind of like people who always want to return to the 'good old days' you know? They think an earlier time is easier, or happier, or whatever. Well I've got news for them. In spite of the problems this world is having, *these* are the good old days. A hundred years from now people will dream romantic thoughts about living in the first years of the twenty-first century, just like people now think there was some magical romance to the world in the late nineteenth century. Our Home World isn't a bad place. You might really like it. But your mother and I think you have a better chance here to do whatever you want. Except fly, of course."

"Fly? You mean like without a plane?"

Willoughby grinned, "I'm just kidding."

Several minutes later they were deep in the mountain pass. Nothing but static was coming over the radio, so Willoughby turned it off.

It was eleven o'clock when they came upon a gas station and motel. Willoughby pulled the car slowly into the motel parking lot. "We'll stay here tonight," he said, "it's better than sleeping in the car. I'll go in and get us a couple rooms. There are two overnight bags in the back, the blue and black ones," he looked back at the girls, "don't wake them just yet."

Arlia moaned softly and lifted her head. She opened her eyes suddenly and looked around as if something was wrong. "We're stopped," she said nervously.

"We're at a motel," Willoughby said.

She let out a relieved breath and settled her head back on the headrest. When Willoughby opened the car door Amy woke up. Carl felt a sudden surge of fear in her when she woke. She looked around quickly, just like Arlia. When she saw who she was with, the panic melted away like snow on warm pavement.

The girls were doing little more than sleepwalking as Arlia helped them to their room. They would wake up in the morning wondering where they were and how they got into those beds. Carl wasn't far behind them, falling onto a squeaky stiff bed, he was asleep before he had a chance to enjoy how truly uncomfortable the bed was.

Willoughby went back out to the car to get his road map. Arlia stayed in the room.

"Willoughby Tennison?"

A man stepped out from the shadows behind the car. Willoughby's heart sank. "Yes," he said to the man.

"I'm here to take you to the rendezvous," the man said.

Rendezvous meant the place where a ship would pick them up for the return to the Homeworld. A ship, or one of the new Displacers. Obviously this man did not have one of those. Willoughby had taken measures to make sure they would not be followed. But since they had been found, it meant he had been watched more closely than he suspected. There was a locator planted somewhere on them, or more likely on the car. It disappointed him to think they had mistrusted him so.

This was a critical moment. The way he reacted to this man would determine how much of a chance they would get to escape. He had to play it cool. He needed this man to think they were running from the Earth Government, not their own.

"Good," Willoughby said. He tried to sound relieved.

"Why didn't you use the beacon?" the man asked. The beacon was the emergency evacuate signal which Arlia could send from her organizer.

"We were separated when they first moved on us," Willoughby said, "we needed to get away quick. And we have an Earth girl with us."

"The Earth girl is unacceptable," the man said.

"I'm aware of that," Willoughby let a note of irritation into his voice. "We were hoping to get away, wait for a while then return her before issuing the beacon." The truth was, by taking Amy they were not only saving her from her Uncle, but saving themselves from the threat of getting zapped back to the Homeworld with one of the new Displacers. There were strict rules against that sort of thing being done in front of Earth people. Rules of course which Arlia had already broken.

The man seemed to think about it for a moment, then nodded. "We noted your use of the Displacer. A bit excessive, but correctable."

"It was necessary," Willoughby said.

"Perhaps."

"We'll return the girl tomorrow. Do you want us to rendezvous back here? Or is there a location near Olympia?"

"Find a location tomorrow night, we'll pick you up when you issue the beacon."

"Okay." Willoughby slid the map under the car seat, stepped out of the car and locked the door. He started to walk casually toward the motel.

"Mister Tennison?" Willoughby stopped and looked at the man. He seemed to be wearing no expression at all. "You had us concerned."

"Why is that?" Willoughby tried to sound as innocent as possible.

"I think you know why," the man said, then turned quickly and disappeared into the darkness. Willoughby hurried into the motel room.

Arlia was lying on the bed, already dozing. Willoughby shook her gently, "wake up."

"What?" she woke suddenly, her eyes wide.

"An Overseer just caught me in the parking lot."

"Ohmygod." Arlia was on her feet, moving toward her organizer.

"It's alright," Willoughby put his hand on her shoulder, "he's gone. I told him we didn't issue the beacon because we had Amy with us and we need to return her first."

"Good." She sat back onto the bed. "What are we going to do?"

"We need to know how they found us. Was your organizer on?"

Arlia slid off the bed and grabbed the organizer. She flipped it open and checked it's display. "No," she said. "And I know it was off earlier, I was showing it to the girls."

"Hmmm. Then there's something in the car."

"I can check it," she said, "won't matter if I turn it on now. They know we're here."

She held the organizer close to her face as she circled the car, trying to read the display in the dim light of the parking lot. She circled the car twice, seeming to find nothing. Then stopped near the back and bent slowly down on her knees. She leaned down and extended the device under the car. "Do you have a flashlight?"

"Yes," Willoughby pulled a small flashlight out of the glovebox, then leaned down next to her and shined it under the car. Attached to the bottom of the gas tank was a tiny silver disk, no bigger than a dime.

"There you go," she said.

"It's pretty clean," Willoughby noticed, "it hasn't been there very long."

"They don't trust us."

"I got that impression. He made a point to tell me they were concerned."

"What do we do?"

"Check the car again. Make sure this is the only one. I think we're still in good shape." Arlia orbited the car four more times, sometimes leaning close to a door or a tire or a fender, but didn't find anything else.

"Okay," he said, "now we get some sleep. Tomorrow we hope for the best." He looked to the sky, trying to spot a shadow moving through the clouds, but saw nothing.

Chapter Twelve

Carl dreamed. He was on a hoverboard, just a little larger than a skateboard, flying across the water of a blue-green lake at almost five hundred miles an hour. The wind slicked his hair back and roared in his ears. James and Norman were hot on his heels. He swerved one way, then the other, kicking up waves of white water. They yelled at him and slowed down. Norman turned too fast and fell off, skipping along the water like a rock.

The lake was several miles wide. Towering cliffs rose hundreds of feet along one shore, like giants rising from the lake. The other shore was tree-lined. Far away, beyond the trees, Carl could see snow capped mountains.

Carl's board came screaming up to the shore where the family was camped. The board skimmed off the water and rode up onto the shore, hovering a couple inches off the ground. Carl slowed quickly to a stop. Candy and Amy were lying on blankets, reading. Willoughby and Arlia were sitting in the grass, watching Carl.

"Did you see Norman wipe out?" he asked his parents. They didn't respond. "Dad?" He glanced over to Candy and Amy, they were looking at him like he was crazy.

"Talking to projections again Carl?" Candy teased, "Not a good sign."

Then he remembered. Mom and Dad were gone. Captured back when they were still on Earth, sent to a mining planet where their brains had been removed and placed in asteroid mining machines. All Carl and Candy had now were projections. Three dimensional pictures of their parents.

"Talking to projections again Carl?" Candy repeated, "Not a good sign." He looked at her, she was fading in and out. A buzzing came from the rocky sand near his feet, a tiny black box with a light shining on one side; a projector. Candy and Amy were suddenly gone. Everyone was gone. Even the sound of the water splashing against the shore had an artificial buzz to it.

"No," he said, "No, I want to go back to Earth. I want things to be like they were before." He heard a rumble and looked back over the lake. A large chunk of the cliff at the far end of the lake had fallen away. It crashed into the water, sending a wave barreling toward Carl. It was over a hundred feet tall. It engulfed him like a thick blanket, blocking out light and crushing him against the shore.

He woke in the dark, wrapped in a sleeping bag on a stiff, squeaky boxspring in a strange motel. The dream should have shaken him, but suddenly all he could think was, I'm going to have to start at a new school some-

121

where, and make new friends. I won't know anyone. I'll probably never see James again. Someday he's going to be getting beat up and I won't be there to stop it.

All the friends he had right now he had made before sixth grade. Since then he had not really gotten to know anyone very well. His head had been buried in books and video games. Whatever life was ahead of him here on Earth, it was just as alien as if they were returning to the Homeworld.

Homeworld … it sounded so mysterious, so fantastic. He wondered what it would be like to go there. To see another planet, and travel through space. A planet with a lavender sky and two suns, how cool is that?

Eventually he fell asleep, but his mind raced with images. Scattered by confusion.

Willoughby woke everyone early. The sun was not yet above the mountains as they climbed into the car, everyone pale and tired. Sleep was like a barrier between one day and the next, like the turning of a page, it made things seem farther away and made strange things seem like dreams. In this case though, the little motel in the mountains, the cool fresh air, and the early hour on the highway reminded everyone of what had happened yesterday.

To everyone's surprise, Willoughby did not turn east toward the glowing sky, but rather west, the direction they had come from "A change of direction," he said. "I thought we'd have breakfast at that little restaurant, and then head down into Oregon. How does that sound?"

He was answered by polite grunts from the back

seat. Candy and Amy looked like they were about to go back to sleep, Carl was just staring straight ahead with a pale, tired expression.

The restaurant was a little family diner at the freeway interchange next to a gas station. It had only been open a few minutes when the Tennisons pulled into the parking lot. They marched inside like sleeping zombies, but perked up when they were greeted with the smell of coffee, bacon, and fresh baked sticky buns.

Willoughby asked for a window seat where he could see traffic coming off the freeway. All during breakfast he watched the cars stopping at the gas station.

Candy and Amy were leaning against each other, still very tired, but other than that they seemed content to be led wherever the family was headed. "I'm not that hungry," Candy said, "I'll just have a sticky bun."

"Me too," Amy said in a little voice.

"They're huge," Willoughby said, "you two could probably share one and still not finish it."

"Okay," they mumbled.

Willoughby ordered biscuits and gravy, Arlia had an egg-white omelet, and Carl had blueberry pancakes.

"I had a dream last night," Carl said around a mouthful of pancake, "I was riding a hoverboard across a lake," he swallowed, looked at his parents to see if they would react, but they seemed more interested in their food. "Do they really have things like that?"

Arlia shrugged her shoulders, "I imagine. I don't really know." She glanced at Willoughby, he was pouring more coffee even though he had only taken a sip.

"I had something like that when I was younger," Willoughby said, "little suicide rockets really. Horrible things to try to control. I imagine they've improved them."

"Could you ride them on water?"

"Not very well. You hit a little chop and it would dive into the water and send you down face first. Not uncommon for kids to get killed trying stunts like that."

"Hmmm," Carl said. He wanted to ask more but he noticed his Mom had stopped eating. Suddenly the omelet had lost it's appeal, she was just poking at it with a fork.

Arlia saw Carl watching her. She tried to act casual, even went so far as to choke down several more bites of breakfast. But the butterflies were churning away inside her. Doubts. She wondered if running away was the right thing for the kids. Maybe they should just give it up and go back home.

When they were done Willoughby handed Arlia some cash, "pay the bill," he said as he stood, "I'll meet you back at the car. C'mon Carl."

The parking lot was damp, as if it had rained late last night, even though it had not. The moisture was probably from someone hosing down the pavement during the night. Willoughby guided Carl to the back of the car and had him kneel down with him. He pointed to the small object attached to the gas tank. "Take a look at that," he said, "that's a tracker. They're using it to follow us."

"Who is? The government?"

"No, our people."

"What do we do?"

Willoughby looked up, toward the freeway. A blue Honda had just pulled off from the Northbound off-ramp and was pulling into the gas station. He reached under the car and pulled the dime-sized object off. He handed it to Carl, "we're going to give it a good home. Hop in the car."

They pulled the car out of the restaurant parking lot into the gas station, pulling to the pump directly behind the blue Honda. "While I fill the tank, you pop that under the bumper of that car. It's magnetic, it'll practically jump out of your hand."

Outside the restaurant, Arlia, Candy and Amy stood next to a newspaper machine, watching the scene at the gas station.

"We can just walk over there," Candy said.

"Never hurts to have them come for you," Arlia said, "and besides …" she pointed to a light pole in a corner of the parking lot. On top was a video camera pointed at the gas pumps. "Who knows who will be looking at that later. It'll confuse them if they see them without us."

Amy was standing with her face pointed skyward, eyes closed, breathing deep. She seemed to be enjoying all this. We've come from opposite directions, Candy thought. The life I knew has crumbled apart, but hers is starting to take a shape.

Arlia giggled. Candy looked over at the gas station. Carl had just done a really bad job of looking innocent as he bent down behind the Honda and planted the tracker.

Nevertheless, the job was done. So long as no one was watching through the security camera.

"Mom?" Candy asked.

"Yes?"

"What's the other world like? I mean, other than the purple sky and the two suns and hoverboards. I mean … is it a lot different than this? A lot more modern?"

"You mean is it like The Jetsons? Huge skyscrapers on pedestals reaching miles into the sky? People flying to work and school. Computer-run society?"

"Yeah. Is it like that?"

"No," she said, "at least, it wasn't last time we were there." She looked up and down the highway, her gaze paused on the forest across the road. "It's not that much different than Earth really. Not as colorful. There's not much labor. Most of the work is intellectual; they put an emphasis on learning, always learning. There are countries just like here, some of them still fight wars against each other. The more advanced nations try to keep technology from the warring ones … to make sure no one can wipe out the planet." She paused for a moment, watching Willoughby and Carl, Candy thought she was done. "There are these two countries," she continued, "which are completely primitive. They've been at war since before our recorded history. Dozens of centuries. They fight with swords, and knives, and hand-to-hand. They've done it for so long that it's become a religion to them. A rite of passage. They don't fight because they hate each other, but because it's part of their lives. It's what they do. Young men and women join when they turn sixteen. If

126

they survive two years of war they are considered adults. We've always expected them to wipe themselves out one day, but they just keep going. Quite the warrior race."

"Weird," Candy said, "what do you mean the world isn't as colorful as this one?"

"A long time ago, when we went through the Industrial Age like this world did, we polluted our world terribly. And we didn't stop in time. A lot of vegetation and animals died, the oxygen content of the air was diminished. Some areas which had been farmlands turned into desert." She looked down at Candy, rested her hand on her shoulder, "this planet feared destroying itself with Nuclear War. We almost destroyed ours through Industrialization. It's been several centuries and we're just now seeing signs that things are coming back. But who knows if it will ever look like this." She stared into the trees for a moment, daydreaming. "Who knows? Maybe it's not really that bad. Maybe I just like it better here. I was seventeen when I left there. I was what you would call a Discontented Youth. I didn't like my government, my society. I was a bit of a rebel I guess."

"So you go to work for your government? Quite the rebel Mom."

Arlia laughed, "yeah, ironic isn't it? I hate my government so I go to work for it. But I let it serve *me* for once. They sent me here, let me start a new life as long as I told them about this world, kept them up to date on what was happening."

"Were they really that bad?"

"I really don't know. I was young, I had a lot of

grand ideas about how the world should be … I thought adults were all stupid. All I know of them is what they were like back then. Maybe – now that I'm an adult, and a parent – I'd think of it differently."

"Have you thought about it?"

"About going back?"

"Yeah."

"Of course. We both did. We thought about it for a combined total of about five minutes. Then we came to our senses and realized we wanted to stay here." She patted Candy on the shoulder. Candy's eyes were locked on a bug crawling across the pavement near her feet. Arlia swallowed hard to keep her breakfast from coming back up. "Do you want to go there Candy?"

Candy didn't answer right away. That in itself was an answer. "I don't know," she said, "it would be interesting. But I don't think I'd want to live there. I like things here. Maybe if I could just go visit sometime, just for a while."

"Yeah," Arlia mused, "well, maybe someday we'll be able to work something out. The future is a big place, anything can happen there. It took us months to get here by ship … but I've heard they can route a Displacer signal now and get there almost instantly."

The station wagon pulled up in front of them. Carl hopped out of the front seat, grinning. "Madam," he said as he held the door open for Arlia.

"Thank you sir," she said, "I see you successfully completed your mission."

"Yes," he said, "the rebels are safe, the empire is

defeated again."

She ruffled his hair, "funny."

They sat in the restaurant parking lot until the Honda was back on the freeway, heading toward Olympia, and probably beyond.

"They'll track it once it goes past Olympia," Willoughby said, "but they won't get close enough to take a look until tonight. Once they see it's not our car we should be well into Oregon."

"My Dad the Spy," Candy teased.

An hour later they were standing in a large bookstore in downtown Portland. Candy and Amy loitered near the magazines while Willoughby searched for road maps. Since breakfast Candy had noticed a change in Amy's mood. Aside from the joy she was feeling being away from her Uncle, there was a feeling like she was holding something back. Wanting to say something but afraid at the same time. As they stood looking at a teen magazine, Candy could feel it bubble up.

"Candy … you know when your mother was talking about you and Carl being able to … sense … what other people were feeling?"

"Yeah?" Candy pretty much knew what Amy was going to ask.

"Can you tell what I'm feeling?" Amy's eyes were open wide, looking a little scared. Maybe it was just curiosity.

"Yeah," Candy said, trying to make it sound like no big deal. "I mean … they talked about being able to communicate that way … but all I can do is get kind of an idea ... you know ... I can't read your mind or anything."

"Okay ... like ... what am I feeling right now?"

Candy opened up a little more, trying to pull more in. Amy's feeling changed almost the moment she asked Candy the question. "You're feeling a little frightened. And it just happened."

Amy's mouth dropped open; she closed it right away. "That's right. I was thinking about my Uncle. Okay, try this one." Amy's eyes went out of focus as she directed all her attention toward thinking about something.

Candy frowned. "That one's tough. It's kind of a mix. A little irritation, a little anger I think, a little bit scared too."

"I was thinking of Andy Bent when I punched him ... this is great." She pointed to a woman about twenty feet away, "what's she feeling?"

The woman was in her early twenties, she was wearing too much makeup, her hair perfectly brushed and sprayed. Her skirt was a little too short for a bookstore early in the morning on a weekday.

"She's scared," Candy said, "but it's a weird kind of scared." She reached more toward the woman, trying to open her mind. She tried something a little different. Something like the relaxation exercise where you relax your feet, relax your legs, relax your back, but she just let it wash over her, like she was letting her muscles go limp. Not enough that she would fall down or anything.

Then it came. Like a wave hitting suddenly when you have your back to the surf. There were hundreds of feelings. Jealousy was the most intense one. It was a

130

strange one to sense, a kind of jealousy Candy had never felt before. It must have been *a grown up* jealousy. The closest thing she could compare it to was the feeling when you realize your best friend likes someone else better than you. Other feelings were flooding in and filling up.

"She's supposed to be meeting someone here," Candy said quietly, "but he hasn't showed. There's a lot of jealousy. She must think he's with someone else."

"That's wild," Amy said.

A tear rolled down Candy's cheek, the emotions were seeping into her. She wasn't just sensing them, she was starting to feel them herself, "She's lonely. She's afraid. She feels like everything she's ever done was a waste of time, and all the good things people have said about her were lies."

"Candy?" Amy said.

"She doesn't have any family around here," Candy was starting to cry openly.

"Candy ... stop it," Amy shook her gently.

"She can't ... help it ... " Candy sobbed, "he promised ... he ... he promised."

Amy shook her harder, "Candy! Stop!" Candy's eyes focused on Amy, she stopped crying, wiped her eyes and fought to breathe normally.

"Wow. I've never done it like THAT." She glanced over at the woman, standing at the end of the magazine racks, thumbing through a magazine as if she were reading it. Candy knew she wasn't. She didn't see a single word on the page. She was feeling the minutes tick by. And every couple seconds she was glancing up and down the aisle, expecting to see someone, and each time she looked up to see no one there; no one except two middle-school girls staring at her. Each time she turned back to the magazine — pretending to read it – it hurt a little worse.

They zigzagged through rows of books, heading back to the front of the store where they were all supposed to meet. There was a small espresso stand there and four round tables. A man in a suit was sitting at a table drinking something brown with ice in it, reading a newspaper.

"Try him," Amy said. "Just don't go too deep."

Candy casually 'flicked' her mind toward him.

Nothing.

She tried a little harder. Still nothing. She reached over and placed her hand on Amy's shoulder for support, just in case she wobbled a little. She tried 'going deep' again. Relaxing, and flexing her mind, but there was nothing there. It wasn't as if he had no feelings, it was as if he wasn't there at all. Like trying to read her Mom and Dad.

It hit her like a brick. "Ohmygod," she whispered. She looked around for the others. None of them were here yet. She grabbed Amy by the wrist and hurried back into the rows of books.

"What is it?" Amy asked.

"Let's find dad."

They raced up row after row, looking for him. Finally they found him — maps tucked under his arm – flipping through a history book about the Civil War.

"Dad," Candy tried to keep panic out of her voice,

"there's a man in the coffee shop ... he ... he doesn't have any feelings ... I ... I mean I can't feel his feelings ... I mean ..."

"I know what you mean Candy," Willoughby glanced the direction they had come as if expecting to see someone after them, "did he see you?"

"I don't think so," she said.

"He didn't," Amy said.

"Is he after us?" Candy asked.

"Probably not," Willoughby said, patting Candy on the shoulder. "He could be one of us, just living here. Or he could be an Earth person. We can't pick up on all of them. Some have other ... problems ... which keep us from feeling them."

"It wasn't like he didn't have any feelings," Candy said, "it was like he wasn't there at all."

Willoughby looked at his watch. "Well, it's time for us to be getting out of here anyway." He closed the history book, carefully slid it back onto the shelf. He checked the maps, still tucked safely under his arm, and hurried toward the front; the girls right on his heels.

Carl had found his way to the Fantasy section. One row ended at a large window which looked out on the sidewalk. In spite of the long, tall rows of books surrounding him, he had become distracted reaching into the feelings of people walking by.

The first had been a dirty little man with a grey scraggly beard. He looked like a homeless person. Carl reached out to him and found many foggy feelings, as if nothing really touched the man. Like a barrier, or a shield, protecting him from the world he walked through. There was sadness there; a hopelessness which made Carl's heart ache and at the same time made him feel tired. Like he just wanted to sit down somewhere, go to sleep and never wake up.

A well dressed older man hurried by. He was tense. He was suffering little stabbing pains in his chest. He was afraid it was a heart attack, but at the same time afraid to ask for help. Carl watched the man as he stopped and leaned against a light pole. He pressed a hand to his chest, scowled, and looked around at the others walking along the street.

Suddenly the man went down, as if his legs had stopped working. Carl turned and sprinted up the aisle, racing toward the cashier at the front of the building. There were two people checking out, he shoved one aside, he didn't notice his family waiting by the front door.

"There's a man on the sidewalk having a heart at- tack!" the cashier gave him a weird look, Carl pointed back toward the fantasy section, "I was back there looking out the window and saw him collapse."

"Just a moment," the cashier said to the customer she was helping. She turned around and picked up the phone. Carl couldn't hear what she was saying, but he could tell from what she was feeling that she had dialed nine one one.

Someone touched his arm, "Carl," it was Candy. "It's time to go."

"But out on the sidewalk …"

"He'll get help," Willoughby said, stepping up be-

134

hind Candy. He glanced back toward the espresso bar, "let's get going."

"But …"

"Now."

They hurried out the door and turned toward the car. Willoughby glanced back once, trying to look casual about it and saw the man staring at them, very intently. He's trying to read us, Willoughby thought.

The car was parked around the corner. They loaded up quickly. Willoughby turned around and headed away from the store to avoid driving by the espresso bar. In minutes they were back on the freeway, heading south. Just four hours from the safety of the Oregon Vortex.

Chapter Thirteen

Jessica rubbed her eyes. They were dry, tired and red. She had been up all night talking on the phone to agents in the area, and the project leads in Geneva.

"Any update from White Pass?" she said into the phone. The room was dimly lit. Portland, Oregon was a beautiful city, but the NSA office here did not have a single window. Just a series of grey cubicles decorated with government calendars and white boards.

"We're just getting satellite information now. It will be maybe an hour before we can determine anything solid."

"Let me know," she clicked the phone off and turned back to the computer. The Chairman was staring out at her from the screen, a dark frown on his face.

"There was aerial activity last night near White Pass," she said. "It will be an hour before we can deduce anything from the satellite photos."

"So," the chairman said, "it is not unlikely that they escaped."

"It's not unlikely," she agreed. "But I'm keeping agents in the area until we're certain."

He grunted, "Keep me informed." His hand moved and the screen went blank.

The only thing on her desk was her open briefcase. Inside it was a thick stack of reports and photos. On top was the Tennison Report. She skimmed it for a while. Part reading and part daydreaming. Background checks and investigator results dating back almost twenty years.

They raised a family here, she thought. It looks like they came here separately, and met here.

She tossed the papers aside and checked out a few of the earlier satellite photos. There had been activity over Olympia in the early morning which had moved toward the Cascade Pass in the evening. She traced the line of the highway with her finger.

"Running," she whispered. "From them and from us. Has to be." She dug down into the bottom of the briefcase, found her road atlas and flipped through pages until she found the map of Western Washington. She looked at the entire area, looking for escape routes.

Eastern Washington? If I was being chased by an alien race, with the ability to watch me from space, I wouldn't flee into Eastern Washington. Too desolate and open, easy to be spotted.

"They're here somewhere," she said to herself, her finger planted firmly over Portland, just across the Columbia River from Washington State. She stared at a dark empty wall for a minute, then pulled her cell-phone from her jacket.

"Willie, this is Sharpe. I want everyone pulled from the borders and passes and moved into Oregon." She flipped pages on her map to bring up Oregon. Her finger slid down the blue and red line of the freeway as it dropped toward California. "Lay out a pattern along I-5, from … say … Eugene to the California border … and cover the Redwood Highway. Meet me here in Portland and we'll flank out." She clicked the phone off, there was a tap at the door, "come in," she said.

An agent in a dark grey suit stepped in carrying several sheets of thin paper. It looked like FAX paper. "We have the information on Amy Nottingham's Uncle," he said.

"Go," she said.

"As reported earlier, we are fairly certain he's native to this planet, even though we found no record of him at all prior to Amy moving in with him after her parents disappeared nine years ago … but after some deeper digging we found this," he handed her a sheet of paper. She scanned it quickly.

"Oh my," her mouth fell open, "I want the field agents to all have this information. If they find the Tennisons I want this to be the first thing they're told."

"Got it."

"Move on it." He turned and hurried out of the room. Jessica stood, carefully reading the reports, shaking her head in amazement.

In a dark bubble inside a large dark shadow submerged beneath Puget Sound, a man sat watching a three dimensional map floating in the air in front of him. A tiny dot moved along grey pavement surrounded by fluorescent green virtual trees and grass.

"Where are you going Willoughby?" he asked as the dot passed Olympia and continued travelling up the freeway. He pressed a small blue dot on his collar, "I need an observation static. Interstate Five, Tacoma. I.D. the Tennison chip as it passes, I want a visual." A soft beep told him his instructions were being followed. He leaned back, watching the dot. Wondering. He pressed the blue dot again, "I want coverage on the Vortex, just in case."

Chapter Fourteen

The freeway was long, straight, and flat. The sky was clear and the air was warm. It was still Summer after all. But here in Oregon it looked more like July than September.

Willoughby and Arlia had been tense and quiet since leaving Portland, but in the last half-hour they had lightened up and started talking. It was feeling more like a vacation than an escape. Carl had his nose buried in a book, while Amy was challenging Candy to read the feelings of people in passing cars. Arlia was trying to teach her how to control it, understand it, and recognize where it came from.

"When people feel things, their brains pump chemicals into their blood to make the feeling stronger. Most of the time the *feeling* you notice is from the chemicals. When you get better at it, you'll be able to dig deeper and really get into their heads. That's where telepathy will come in."

Candy thought about the woman at the bookstore. "Telepathy sounds freaky," she said. "Being able to read people's minds ... I'm not sure I'd want to do it."

"Well," Arlia said. "You don't really read minds. You send and receive thoughts. People only hear what you send. The problem on Earth is that most people are sending their thoughts all the time without knowing it ... it's very noisy."

"That's why we don't do it here," Willoughby said. "You open your mind to it and it's like sticking your head in a jet engine. Way too much noise."

Candy wondered what it would be like to reach into Amy's mind. Work into the corners and find out what the real story was with her Uncle. What had gone on there. What made her so afraid.

Amy glanced at Candy, then looked away embarrassed. "I'm sorry ... I was just thinking about my garden," she told her. "All those cucumbers ..."

"Oh my ..." Willoughby said. "That *is* sad. Cucumbers should never go to waste like that."

Amy smiled. She turned to Candy, "I'm fine," she insisted. She pointed at a car as it passed. "How about that one? What are they feeling?"

A lot of what Candy had been sensing in the cars was boredom. People heading down to California, bored by the long straight freeway, not even noticing the aquablue mountains in the distance, or the sparse puffs of bright white clouds dotting the sky like cotton balls. Some were playing loud music, blocking out the outside world. Some were talking about nothing at all, boring the others

141

in the car. Some were angry, one was arguing as they drove. A wife was shouting and the husband was ignoring her.

The car Amy pointed at was a little blue car driven by a lone man with long hair. He was slouched in his seat. Candy reached, but couldn't feel anything. She closed her eyes, took a deep breath and tried again.

"Nothing," she said, "I don't detect anything." That caught Carl's attention. His head came up from his book to follow the car as it passed them.

"Is he one of us?" Carl asked.

Willoughby stared at the car for a moment, then said, "No, he's from Earth."

"So why can't I feel him?" Candy asked.

Arlia frowned, "He's withdrawn. Bad things are going on in his life, or he had a bad upbringing. Could be any number of things. He's given up. He still has feelings, but they don't get out."

"That must be strange," Candy said.

"It's probably a very lonely feeling," Arlia said.

"If you can pick up buried feelings," Willoughby said, "you'll know more about him than he knows himself."

Eventually the road began to wind, and hills rose up around them. "Anyone need a rest area?" Willoughby asked as they passed a sign.

"Right here," Candy and Amy said together, and giggled. Carl carefully placed the bookmark in his book, closed it and set it on the floor. That was as close as he would come to saying he needed a rest area.

The rest area was like an oasis in the desert. If there was a big war and all the cities were destroyed, a person could live off this rest area. It had vending machines selling pop, juice, and snacks. And in the restroom you didn't have to touch anything. All the toilets were what Carl called "stomp aways." You just walked away from it and it would flush. Place your hands under the faucet at the sink and the water would turn on, then place your hands under the air dryer and it would come on. No need to touch anything but the door, and that was easy to kick open.

Carl was in and out of the men's room quick. He knew the girls would take a while, he could hear them giggling. Arlia and Willoughby had wandered to a picnic table and spread out their maps. Other than talking about the Redwood Highway they really had no idea where they were headed or where they would end up. It was scary, but kind of exciting too.

There was a travel kiosk up a path from the restrooms. Maps, advertisements, and vending machines. Pop and candy. Carl was craving a cola and a candy bar.

As he stepped up to the kiosk, he heard a pop can fall down the chute in one of the machines. He rounded the corner and saw a boy his age bending down, pulling out a pop can. Something clicked in Carl's head, and everything seemed to get very quiet. He had the urge to run. No reason for it, he thought. He turned and looked back toward his parents. They were at the picnic table, looking calm, relaxed. A faint echo of giggling came from the restroom, the girls were still there. He turned back, and the boy was facing him. It was James Morlana.

"James?" Carl's eyes grew wide, his breath caught in his throat. James looked calm, like he had been expecting Carl to show up.

"Hi Carl," James said in a matter-of-fact way, as if they were at school. Normal except that in addition to the pop, James was holding a pocket organizer, a little smaller, but otherwise exactly like the one in Arlia's purse.

Candy glanced at the mirror as she washed her hands. Just checking to make sure nothing was smeared on her chin or stuck in her teeth. It struck her then, looking at herself. That girl in the mirror – that face staring back at her — was the face of an alien. She half expected to see antennae rise up from the back of her head, or tentacles sprout from her neck. The girl in the mirror looked normal enough. But she wasn't normal was she? Not by a long shot. Her parents were from another planet. She could read minds. There were probably hundreds of things going on in her body which would never happen in Amy's body. Maybe she had an extra organ? Maybe her blood was different? Maybe she would never age? Or maybe in thirty years her skin would suddenly peel off like a snake and she would have a new body and look young again?

Or maybe in thirty years she'd be living in a cage somewhere under the New Mexico desert. A test subject for government scientists.

Those were heady thoughts. Too much to think

about right now. Right now the important thing was clean hands and well brushed hair. Oh, and nothing stuck in the teeth. She grinned wide for the mirror, holding back the urge to make a scary alien face. I'm not a scary alien, she thought, at least I hope not.

"What are you doing here?" Carl asked.

"I can ask you the same thing," James said, "What *are* you doing here?"

Again the silence. Carl tried to read James's feelings. He reached deep, into the root like his mom had told Candy to do. But he couldn't lock onto anything. It was as if James wasn't really there. It was …

Incredible. James was one of *them*. An alien.

"How long have you known?" Carl asked.

"Known what?" James asked.

"What you are? Where you're from?"

"Where I'm from? I'm from Olympia, just like you. But what I am? I've just known a little while; over the summer. Freaky isn't it? I wish I had known you were too … I had a million questions." Silence. "How did you handle it?"

"I just found out yesterday," Carl said, "I haven't … handled it … yet."

James shook his head as if to say 'yeah, I know what you mean.' "We're all supposed to go back Carl. Why are you guys running? Don't you want to see it? Aren't you curious?"

"No," Willoughby said. Carl jumped and turned around. Willoughby was right behind him. Arlia was hur-

145

rying over from the picnic table, the maps were folded and tucked under her arm. The girls were coming out of the restroom.

James suddenly stood up straight, shoulders back, the organizer held in his right hand. He was nervous. His hand was shaking a little.

"Tell your dad," Willoughby said to James, "that we don't want to hurt anyone. We're not going to talk to anyone, or give away any information. We just want out. We want to live our lives here. If we live normal lives without contact with the Homeworld again, there should be no reason for us to draw anyone's attention … that's all we want."

James looked frightened. After all, he was only fifteen. His eyes were darting from Willoughby to Carl. Willoughby noticed the organizer in his hand, he nudged Carl. "Get in the car," he said, "Hurry."

James took a deep breath, and tried to steady his hand, "I can't let that happen Mister Tennison," he said. He raised the organizer, "I'm sorry."

"RUN!" Willoughby screamed. He reached for Carl, to pull him back, just as James pressed a button on the organizer.

FLASH!

It was like several strikes of silent lightning. Everyone was blinded. "Get down!" Arlia was screaming. She had her Displacer in her hand. "Stop it James!" she yelled. Through flashes of red and orange dots she saw Willoughby and the girls flat on the ground, but not Carl. No sign of Carl.

"NOOOO!!" she screamed. It was the scream of an injured animal, "CARL!!!! NOOOO!" James pointed his Displacer at the girls, but Arlia pressed her button first. The silent lightning returned, and James was gone. She dropped to her knees, her eyes open wide, filling with tears. She started shaking.

"Arlia," Willoughby said, "can you track their signal? Can you tell where they sent Carl?"

Her shaking fingers danced across the pad, pressing buttons, searching for the signature of James's Displacer, she wiped tears from her eyes so she could see clearly. "Yes," she said, "yes I see it." Then her eyes closed painfully. An agonized moan came from deep inside her. She doubled over and began to cry. "No no no no …"

Willoughby leaned down and took the Displacer from her hand. He read the display. "Oh no."

Chapter Fifteen

Carl turned to run. He saw his dad, then a bright flash. Suddenly the ground was gone and he fell. He put his hands down to brace himself, but when he landed he wasn't on the path, or in the grass. It was a floor. A hard floor. Too many things were different all at once. The air was thin and odorless where seconds ago it had smelled like grass and dirt and automobile exhaust. It was easier to breathe. As he stood he felt lighter. It was hard to balance. He started to sway on his feet, then someone grabbed him.

"Portea, lon Carl," a woman's voice, soft and caring. Her words made no sense.

The red, orange and purple dots across his eyes began to fade, making it easier to see. He was standing on a high balcony looking out over a huge city. Tall cylindrical buildings all white or mirrored stretched hundreds of feet into the air. The sky was lavender, giving everything a pale lavender tint. The sun was shining on the horizon directly ahead of him, but he felt the heat of sunlight on the back of his neck as well. He looked back and saw another sun high in the sky behind him.

"Home World," he said. The woman agreed. She didn't say anything, but he knew. Somehow she had understood what he said and told him he was right. It confused him. There was other information too but he couldn't understand it. More was coming, much more, filling his head with ideas, but none of it made sense. He closed his eyes and pressed his hands to his ears. It didn't stop. "No," he said, "No … please …"

Then it stopped.

He opened his eyes slowly. The woman was still there. She looked like his mother, the same age. His heart raced. Could she be his Mom's sister? His aunt?

A relative. An actual living relative.

She held up a small clear tube curved in the shape of a small "c." She pointed it at his ear. "Nara," she said.

He nodded. She fit it to his ear. It wrapped around the outside, just like the end of a pair of glasses would fit. One end curved into his ear.

"Does that hurt?" she said. It sounded strange. He could still hear the words of that strange language; her lips moved to those words, but the tube was broadcasting English into his ear. "It's a translator," she said, "so you can understand me without telepathy." She patted him on the shoulder. "It's just a temporary measure until we teach you to telepath." She extended her hand in greeting, "My name is Tam. I'm your grandmother."

149

"Please tell me he's in Denmark," Candy cried. Willoughby was leading them back to the car, they were running. Candy was terrified. Suddenly this adventure had taken a very serious and unwanted turn. Carl was gone. Carl, her protector.

Candy and Amy fell into the back seat. Willoughby helped Arlia into the front then got behind the wheel and hurried onto the freeway. Arlia was crying, her body shaking.

Tears were running from Candy's eyes, "where did he go Dad?" she begged.

"Home," Willoughby said flatly. He didn't have to explain, she knew he didn't mean Olympia.

She felt Amy's arm around her. Amy was afraid, but she was more afraid for Candy than herself. Candy could sense it, she looked at Amy and nodded her head, "I'm okay," she said.

"He's okay," Willoughby said. Candy wasn't sure if he was talking to her or to Mom. Probably both. She figured he was okay, that didn't bother her. He wasn't here with them, that's what bothered her. She wanted him back, or – she realized – she wanted to be there with him.

"Where are we going?" Candy asked.

"South," Willoughby said, "into the vortex. The farther south we go the harder it will be for them to track us. And in about an hour we'll be too deep for them to use the Displacer again."

The car was silent for the next hour. Silent except

for the whine of the tires on the road, the rumble of the engine, and sometimes the sound of Arlia crying. After an hour the crying stopped and she sat staring out the windshield. She looked like she was thinking deeply about something, perhaps about whether or not she wanted to continue running now that Carl was gone. From what they had told her of the Homeworld, she didn't think it sounded so bad that she would trade life on Earth for life without her brother.

I want to go with him – she thought – but she didn't say anything. She sat in the back seat with Amy, looking out the window, waiting for her parents to make a decision. But the road passed under them, that rest area got farther and farther behind them, and no one said anything.

Chapter Sixteen

"Are you too warm?" Tam asked. Carl shook his head. She had brought him a chair and insisted he sit down even though he felt fine. "I know this can be disorienting. You were brought here with a Displacer, your friend James did it. Your parents and sister are all fine, they're still on Earth," she ran her fingers through his hair in a very grandmotherly way, "does all this make sense to you?" he nodded. "Do you know why your parents are running?" Her voice grew soft, as if she was afraid someone was listening. He looked around but they seemed to be alone on the terrace.

"They don't want to come back here," he said, "they just want us to be left alone."

Tam nodded her head slowly but didn't say anything.

"What are you going to do with me?" he asked. He was battling mixed feelings. This was another planet. Lighter gravity, a lavender sky, two suns, modern buildings and probably unbelievable technology all around him. The Homeworld. It was as faraway and new as he could get from the life he knew, but he was here without his family. He was here alone, with a relative he had never known. His parents were probably worried, and Candy was probably terrified.

"What are we going to do with you?" Tam said, "what do you want us to do with you?"

It couldn't be as simple as that. "Send me back," he said.

Her eyebrows rose in surprise, "Just like that?" she snapped her fingers, "you don't want to take a look around first? Visit your Homeworld a little. See where your parents came from and what it is they don't want to come back to?"

It was like she was reading his mind. Which made him wonder if maybe she was. Yes, he did want to see it, all of it. But he wanted to be back with his parents too.

Tam looked away, toward the city. Her eyes lost focus as if she were listening to something which only she could hear. Then she turned back to Carl. "We don't keep prisoners here, Carl, but we don't interfere with alien worlds either. That's why your parents are supposed to come back. We won't force them to stay here, they just can't stay on Earth anymore. There are other worlds if they would like a new assignment."

Other worlds? Other than this one and Earth? How many habitable planets are out there? How many could he visit if he wanted to?

"Your situation is a little confusing," Tam said, "for

us as well as you. Genetically you're one of us, but by birth and upbringing you're an Earth native. So let's make a deal. Spend a couple days here with us. Let us show you this world, introduce you to its people, and try to make you understand our side of your parent's situation. Then we'll send you back. You can stay here if you like, you can stay there if you like. But either way we want you to deliver a proposal to your parents. Does that sound alright?"

Carl was fifteen years old. An early twenty first century teenager. He had a natural tendency to distrust an adult making an offer which sounded too good to be true. This was his grandmother, true enough, and from what he was hearing there seemed to be no downside to their offer. So why were his Mom and Dad so desperate to stay away from here? Why was it so important for them to run? Why were they risking so much?

"Okay," he said.

"Good!" she clapped her hands. "Alright, first off I'll take you home so we can work on your telepath ability. Do you know what I'm talking about?"

"I think so."

"Can you read people a little? Even when you're not trying?"

"Yeah."

"How long have you been able to do that?"

"Uh … I don't know, maybe since I was eight."

"Good … good. Sounds like everything is alive and well and waiting to be tapped."

Carl was nervous about telepathy. It seemed like something overwhelming. Something frightening. "Do we have to do that right away?"

Tam guided him out of the chair, and put her arm around him. "Yes Carl, and once you're doing it you'll understand why. The telepath ability is the root of everything you will see here. It's the reason we haven't destroyed ourselves with war."

"Except for the people who still kill each other with swords?"

She grinned, "I see your parents have not totally shielded you from your heritage. That's good. But I hope they've told you more than just that."

"Not much," he said, "we didn't know we were from here until yesterday."

"Oh my," she said, a bit startled, "then you're feeling some culture shock aren't you?" she took him by the hand and led him into the building, "there's no time to waste. Let's get going."

There was no doorway separating the balcony from the room they entered. It opened into a round room with no furnishings. The walls, floor and ceiling were all made of the same solid-colored light-grey material. His shoes made no sound on the floor as he walked. Ahead of them was a door which slid open as they approached; it looked like an elevator.

"So, what is this place?" he asked.

"Just a meeting place," she said, "we didn't know how many of you we would get, or what mood you'd be in when you got here. So we chose this place because it's fairly secure. Much more so than popping you right into my living room."

They stepped into the elevator, the door closed and opened again before he had time to turn around. Tam stepped back out. Was something wrong with the elevator? He started to follow her, then stopped in surprise. The empty grey room was gone. They were in a well decorated room with open doors at the far end looking out on a small lake and distant trees.

"My house," she said, "welcome."

A Displacer – he realized – it wasn't an elevator at all. It was like the thing which had brought him here from Earth. Of course. People who could transport instantly from one solar system to another wouldn't bother driving from one place to another on their own planet.

"Are you hungry?" she asked.

He hadn't thought about it, but he was. He never had the chance to get anything from that snack machine at the rest area. "Yes," he said.

She stepped over to a wall panel which looked like an entertainment center. He was certain though that he wasn't looking at VCRs or CD players. She pressed a couple spots on a clear black pad, then his stomach felt strange. Like it was expanding. Like he had to burp really bad … or throw up.

He burped. Loud. It tasted like turkey.

"Is that enough?" Tam asked.

"What happened?"

"You just had two turkey sandwiches and a glass of milk predigested and deposited in your stomach. But if you'd prefer to chew and swallow, we can do that too."

"Uh … no … no, that's fine." he rubbed his stomach, hoping to settle it down. Otherwise he was certain he would puke.

She guided him to the terrace. He stepped to the edge and looked down. About ten feet below, a green yard sloped to the edge of the lake perhaps fifty yards away. The lake itself was a couple hundred yards across, it was hard to tell. The tinting of the colored sky and lighting of the two suns made it hard to perceive things the same way he had on Earth. Something darted from one edge of the lake and caught his attention. It looked like someone skiing, but there was no boat. It was a girl, maybe his age or a little older, riding a board across the water. It was a scene right out of his dream. "A hoverboard," he said, awed.

"I think they call them Hummers," Tam said, "but yes, they hover."

"Across water and land?" he asked.

"Yes," she said, "would you like to try it?"

His eyes widened, his pulse raced, "Can I? Really?"

"Sure," she said, "but not until after our first lesson."

"Lesson?"

"Telepathy," she said, "we need to start with that. You'll need it for that," she pointed to the girl on the lake, "as much as anything else. It'll all make sense very soon. Oh, and before I forget …" she reached into her pocket and pulled out a round white patch. She took his right hand, rolled up his sleeve and stuck the patch to the inside of his forearm. He looked at it curiously. It stuck to his skin, but it didn't feel sticky.

"Inoculant," she said.

He looked at her quizzically.

"Like a shot, I guess," she said, "to keep you from getting sick. Lots of microbes here your body has never been exposed to."

"I don't get sick." he said.

"Not on Earth. Your Mom and Dad inoculated you against all known Earth illnesses. But I don't imagine they bothered covering you against ours ... especially since they weren't planning on ever coming back."

Chapter Seventeen

Candy and Amy sat inside the fast-food restaurant while Willoughby and Arlia sat in the car discussing what to do next. Amy had already devoured a large cheeseburger and was almost done with her fries. Candy wasn't hungry. She forced down three fries and felt like she would throw up if she ate anything else.

"Are you going to eat your burger?" Amy asked as she swallowed her last fry.

"I'm not very hungry," Candy said, "you want it?"

Amy had a bite taken out of it before Candy could reach down to hand it to her. It was nice to know Amy had an appetite.

Candy looked out at the car. Willoughby and Arlia had been talking for a long time. Now they were eating, not talking at all. Candy was sick to her stomach with worry about Carl. She wanted him back, or else she wanted to go wherever he was. Her parents saw her watching them and waved for her to come back out to the car.

"Let's go," she said. She was out the door before Amy could wrap up her burger. She dove into the back seat with wide eyes, hoping her parents had come up with a plan for finding Carl. That's what parents were supposed to do right? Come up with the perfect plan in a difficult situation?

"We don't think they're going to keep Carl," Willoughby said, "unless Carl decides on his own he wants to stay." Arlia was staring out the windshield, Willoughby was turned around in his seat so he could talk to the girls. "He's a natural born Earth native, and they're very ethical when it comes to natives. They'll give him the choice."

"But where will they put him? Back at the rest area?" Candy didn't know how to feel. Happy that Carl might come back? Or worried that he'd be set down in the middle of nowhere with no one to help him?

"Probably," Willoughby said, "but they'll give him some way to try to find us, or for us to know he's back," he looked at Arlia, she didn't move. "In the meantime, we're going to keep moving."

Candy said nothing, just looked back and forth at her parents. Amy had her burger unwrapped, merrily chowing away, hardly listening. Willoughby turned around, started the car, and backed out of the parking space.

"What if they don't send Carl back?" Candy asked. "Do we just go on without him?" Her voice was pleading, tears were rising in her eyes.

"We're pretty sure he'll come back," Willoughby said, "if nothing else they'll send him back with a message for us. An offer to come home."

"But if they don't?"

"Then we have to think about going back. We'd like to stay here. But we're not willing to break up the family to do it."

"Good," Candy said. After a pause she added, "I don't care where we go or what we do, as long as Carl is with us." Arlia turned around and reached back to hold Candy's hand. There were tears in their eyes, an understanding even though neither said anything.

"Close your eyes," Tam said, "and think about the lake. You're floating over the lake. Right over the middle of it, high enough that you can see all of it at once."

"Okay," Carl said.

"No," she said, as if she were in his mind with him, "don't think of one spot. Don't think about the Hummers or the sun or how high up you are. Just visualize the entire lake."

It was only a mental exercise, not like he was moving or anything, but he was starting to breath hard; like he had been running. "Okay," he said.

"You can see everything that goes on in or around the lake now, can't you?"

"Yes."

"And if you want to, you can pay attention to one thing without blocking out all the others, right?"

"Uh … yes."

"Okay … blank," she said. This was the signal for him to stop the exercise and completely blank out his mind. Blanking the mind – he had learned – was an extremely difficult thing to do. His brain always wanted to be thinking something, and no matter how hard he tried to blank out everything, little things would creep in. Candy and Mom and Dad, or James during that last instant before the flash hit him, or the distant whooshing sound of a hummer speeding across the surface of the lake.

"You're not blank," Tam said.

Sweat was beading up on his forehead ... no, don't think about that ...

"You're not blank."

Whoosh ... a buzzing somewhere ... Tam moving in her seat ...

"You're not blank."

Blank. It came quickly, it didn't last long.

"Read my feelings," Tam said, "the way you would with an Earth person."

"I can't read you," Carl said.

"Try."

Carl opened his mind. He tried it the way his Mom had been teaching him, reaching out, feeling around the person, reaching into them. But he couldn't find Tam. When he closed his eyes it was like she wasn't there. "I can't find you," he said.

"Open your eyes." She was sitting directly in front of him, their knees were almost touching. Cupped in her hands was a black ball, the size of a softball. It was completely black, no light reflected off it at all. It seemed to only exist on one dimension, as if it had been cut out of a piece of paper, but he could see from the way it sat on her hands that it had height and depth. It was kind of disturbing to look at.

"Okay," she began, "I want you to do that exercise again. Try to reach out and read me. When you feel comfortable with where you are, reach out and place your hands on the orb. This will show you how to step past the block which keeps you from reading me. You can't read my emotions the way you can read Earth people, but you can open a channel of communication. It's much different, much deeper, and it might scare you at first. But this is very important. There is absolutely nothing to be afraid of. Nothing bad is going to happen to you. It's going to be like the exercise with the lake. You'll sense many people, most of them very far away, you'll need to focus your attention on me without losing the connection to them."

"Will they be reading my mind too?"

She shook her head, "it's not mind reading. It's telepathic communication. You will detect other people, but you can't hear them unless they want to be heard. And they can't hear you unless you want to say something."

He nodded, even though he wasn't quite sure what she was talking about. It scared him to think that in a couple minutes he might understand. He wasn't sure he wanted to understand.

"Would you like some water before you begin?" she asked. He nodded. She got up and walked over to the panel. He felt a surge of panic remembering the *pre-digested* turkey which had suddenly filled his stomach earlier.

"Could I drink it?" he asked.

She nodded, a hint of a smile on her lips, and stepped out of the room.

Perhaps it was an alien premonition deep in his mind, but he felt like he was standing at the base of a dam, watching cracks form in the concrete, knowing a huge ocean of water was about to crush him.

Tam returned quietly to the room, her footsteps made no sound on the floor. She handed him a small paper cup. It felt empty but it was filled with water. He drank eagerly. It was cold and fresh; he could feel it all the way down. It was a tiny cup, but he felt like he had just drank several glasses. He handed her the empty cup, she crushed it in her hand and it was gone! Vanished.

"Decomposed," she said, "microscopic particles fall from my hand to the floor. Later the housecleaning system will pick it up and return its particles into the house maintenance system. Tomorrow its particles might be another cup, or part of a meal, or a new pair of socks."

She was sitting in front of him again, knees almost touching. She had been holding the orb in one hand, now she cupped it in both again.

"Okay. Start with a blank mind. Then read me, and touch the orb."

Blank. It was easier than before. Although still not easy.

Reaching. Searching. Trying to stretch his mind toward Tam, then he reached his hands out and touched the orb.

WHAM!!

He opened his eyes. He was on the floor, Tam was standing over him. "Are you alright?" He tried to nod, he wasn't sure if he did or not. "Do you have to be sick again?" Sick? He couldn't remember being sick. He shook his head. She was helping him up, guiding him back into the chair. "I apologize. You're stronger than I thought. We need to use the orb differently."

The light outside was different. Not as bright. Almost normal. "Tara has set," she said, "you were out for about an hour." He had never heard the proper names but somehow he knew Tara was one of the two suns; the other was Tiru. Givers of life. Good and evil forever battling in the heavens for a dominance neither would ever have. In the ancient nation of Bitru-lee where people still died in an endless war fought with swords, the suns of Tara and Tiru were etched on their shields. And when the bodies of the dead were burned to cinders in open fields it was thought their essence joined the battle in the sky. He knew all this somehow. A transfer of knowledge from his contact with the orb. He knew the borders of Bitru-lee were closed, no one passed to or from the country any longer, but it was rumored that modern people – unhappy with their lives – entered Bitru-lee with Displacers and joined the ancient war to bring meaning to their lives. Most of society frowned upon it as an easy way to commit suicide.

Tam was holding another cup of water. He drank it eagerly. It was just as refreshing as the first. Water condensed directly from the atmosphere just seconds before he drank it. As pure as any water could possibly be.

He crushed the cup in his hand and felt it disappear.

"Okay," Tam said. She was in front of him again, the orb in her hands. "This time we're going to do it a little differently. I don't want you to do anything but go blank. I will guide us into it through the orb. You'll know when to take control. If anything goes wrong I will break the contact. Okay?"

He nodded. He realized he had not spoken since he woke up on the floor, but his head was filled with new information. Like having been in school for years, but learning it all in one second. Even now, as he sat here, he could feel his brain still learning things from the brief contact with the orb. It was freaky. But it was really cool too.

"Blank," Tam said.

He went blank. It was easy, and he managed to hang onto the *blankness* with confidence.

He wasn't aware of Tam touching him, or touching the orb. But suddenly he heard something, or felt something, or both. Like many voices far away. He could tell they were voices but he couldn't tell what they were saying.

Tam was communicating, but not with speech. She was teaching him, the way a computer would download a large file. He could feel his head filling with new things.

Sense the voices. She was telling him. And he did. He pulled back from the voices just as he had pulled back from the lake.

Find my voice, she said. And he did. It was close, and strong, and reaching for him. It was the only voice

166

reaching for him. Like spotting a blue light in a sea of white.

Teach me about apples, she said. He thought about an apple. *No. Not the word. Don't tell it, think it, and send me the thoughts.* In his mind he created a pool of apple. The essence of it, the feeling of it, his history of it. It was like a package. Everything he had ever known about apples in one little corner of his mind, bundled like a package, then sent to Tam.

Good, she said, *very very good. Now I'm going to give you a connection. Don't be afraid.* He sensed her essence coming closer. Then it was all around him.

Perception. Suddenly he wasn't sitting there. He was in Tam's head. Feeling the world from behind her eyes. Everything was different. He saw this world the way she saw it. He saw the room the way she saw it. It was no longer a new, strange room on a strange world. It was a familiar room, with much history. Very comforting. It was home. It had been home for a long time. He knew how to work the food panel. He knew where the bedrooms were and when the sheets had been changed … and …

… he saw himself. Not as Carl Tennison, High School Student. But as Carl, the grandson Tam had never seen. The grandson she thought she would never see. He thought of himself as a grown-up, she thought of him as a young man with much still to learn. And beyond that … Mom. But she wasn't Mom. She was a baby, a toddler, a little blonde girl laughing down by the lake, riding a Hummer for the first time, crashing into the far shore and bouncing halfway up the shore toward a neighbor's house.

Mom ... Arlia ... on her first day of school. Using the orb for the first time. Arlia in her teen years ... rebelling from authority. Tam worried. Tam afraid what her daughter might do. Then pain. Arlia gone. Gone to Earth. More pain. Arlia breaking more rules, marrying a man named Willoughby, a man Tam had never met. Brief notes from Earth, rare gifts. Loneliness. Crying.

And sudden discovery, like a light bulb coming on. Here he was sitting in the same room with Tam, but from behind their eyes they each saw it as a different room. This was what caused so much pain and misunderstanding on Earth. There was no way for one person to experience something exactly the same way as someone else. Everyone looked at things through their upbringing, their experience, their likes and dislikes, their wants and needs. And no two could be exactly alike. A small thing to one person could be a big deal to another, and neither person could possibly understand where the other was coming from. Such isolation. And it could only lead to conflict.

Arlia and Tam were together the moment Arlia's assignment to Earth was announced. Arlia busted with excitement, Tam collapsed in agony. The same moment, but two different moments for two different people. The difference between this world and Earth was that these people could share those feelings. They could share each other's lives in exact detail. There was no chance of misunderstanding. No chance of not knowing what the other person felt. It was perfect, flawless communication.

And it hurt.

It was gone. He opened his eyes, the room was blurry from the tears in his eyes. He wiped them away. Tam was still in front of him, she was setting the orb on the floor. When she sat up he saw tears in her eyes too. He leaned forward and reached for her. They sat there for some time; hugging and crying.

Chapter Eighteen

Grants Pass, Oregon was in Southern Oregon, smack in the middle of the Oregon Vortex, and the city where the Redwood Highway broke off from the freeway. Willoughby had been driving around for several hours checking out Used Car lots. Finally he found a van in pretty good shape that they could afford. The family waited in the car while he dealt with the salesman, paying cash for the van. Candy didn't know how much money they had, she didn't want to know. It would be one more thing to worry about. And besides, money was an adult worry. They wouldn't be on the run if they couldn't afford it. Would they?

It was getting dark as they got back on the freeway; Arlia drove the car, Willoughby led in the van. Candy was confused. "I thought we were taking the Redwood Highway?"

"We will," Arlia said, "we're going to try confusing anyone who might be following us too close."

After a couple miles they took an exit which looked isolated. Up a narrow two-lane road they pulled onto a wide spot on the road. Arlia opened her Displacer and began tapping away. Willoughby moved all their belongings from the car to the van. Candy and Amy climbed into the back. There was a bench seat in the back, but two captain's chairs in the middle with a round table between them and a large tinted window out the driver's side. It was pure luxury compared to the old station wagon.

"Where's the TV?" Amy teased. Candy grinned.

Out the windshield she watched Arlia slide the Displacer under the station wagon then run back to the van. Seconds later came the bright flash; and the old wagon was gone. Her Displacer was still lying on the pavement. She retrieved it and ran back to the van. Willoughby got behind the wheel and in minutes they were back on the freeway.

Candy pointed at the Displacer, "I thought you said that didn't work around here?"

"It works," Arlia said, "but not very well, and it's hard to trace. They know we just used it, but it'll take them a while to find where, and then to trace where it went."

"So they'll think we escaped?"

"That's the idea."

"Will it work?"

"No," Willoughby said, "but it'll buy us some time. Give us a little breathing room."

"So our car is in Denmark?"

"No," Arlia said, "that's where I sent James

171

Morlana," there was obvious anger in her voice when she mentioned James, "he would tip them off right away if our empty car suddenly appeared … if he's still there. The vortex messes up the settings, but if it worked right, our car is in Tibet."

"Probably in the middle of a mountain," Willoughby added.

"Yes. Or it popped in the middle of the air and fell to the ground." Candy's eyes widened. Arlia grinned, "that's why we wouldn't really use it to escape. It's not that reliable here."

"But Carl …" Candy began.

"Is safe," Arlia finished. "They've advanced the technology since they gave me this," she tapped the Displacer, "he's on the Homeworld. Probably with your grandmother."

"Grandmother?"

"It's a long story."

They were off the freeway again. On a highway heading southwest, into the Redwoods, and hopefully safety.

"It was identical to the signal we traced the night Hennesey disappeared," the agent said. Jessica was sitting next to him, in the back of a government car heading south on the freeway toward a rest stop which had displayed something odd on a satellite survey photo just hours earlier.

"What's the status in the area?" she asked.

"Local authorities have the license number and de-

172

scription of the car."

"And the Nottingham information?"

"The media has it. It will be in all the local papers in the morning."

"Is there some way we can get it out there so we're sure they get it?"

"You want to try local radio?"

"Would that be too obvious?"

"It's going to make local news anyway. If we try something specifically targeted toward them we might look desperate. That would put up red flags, and in that part of the state we're likely to find a lot of backwoods people crawling out of the brush to help them. Better to let it develop as a victim story."

Jessica watched the scenery pass by. Cars. Cars everywhere. Everyone doing something, going somewhere. For a moment she wondered if everyone they passed was from this planet. How many of them are out there? How high up in our society have they infiltrated? For all she knew the members of the council could all be aliens, just playing her for a fool to draw attention away from themselves. Maybe we don't really want them for research. Maybe they're victims of an alien conspiracy right here on our own planet, and we're helping them get rid of their problems.

She grinned. Impossible. Well, not impossible, but not bloody likely. At least she hoped not.

Her cell-phone rang. "Sharpe," she said. Her brows tightened, her lips grew taunt, then a little grin. "Mail me the details when you've got them," she hung up.

"Good?" the agent asked.

"Found the people we lost this morning," she paused for effect, "… in Denmark."

"Amazing," the agent shook his head.

"More than you think. They were climbing onto a helicopter when they got an unexpected visitor. An Olympia High School student … friend of Carl Tennison's. He didn't seem too surprised to be there, but wasn't happy to see us."

Chapter Nineteen

Carl's head was spinning. He felt like he had crammed six years of school into just a few seconds of telepathy with Grandma Tam. His head was full of stuff he didn't expect, or understand. He didn't even know it was there until he started thinking about it. When he wondered where this planet was ... he knew. He could point it out on a map of the galaxy. The problem was, he had no idea what Earth astronomers called the stars which he now knew by the names used on this planet. He knew he was very far from Earth. The other side of the galaxy. An impossible distance.

His parents came to Earth the old fashioned way; by space ship. Twenty years ago they departed their Homeworld and traveled through a series of wormholes which eventually led to Earth's Solar System.

Recently a way had been found to channel a Displacer signal through the wormholes with a series of relays. Nothing much bigger than a person could travel this way, so the spaceships already in Earth's solar system stayed there. They were needed as transformers to direct the Displacer signals toward the wormholes.

There was a lot of complicated science involved, and whether he understood it or not, it was right there in his head. He knew it all. He couldn't build a Displacer out of pop cans and bubble gum, but he could probably fix a broken one if he had the right tools.

Telepathy was an amazing thing. If teachers on Earth could do it there would be no need for tests. No need for twelve years of school. On this planet it only took students a matter of hours to learn everything an Earth child would learn in twelve years. And even then, they continued their education into early adulthood; learning everything they could possibly learn, from anyone who knew something they wanted to know. A kid his age on this world had more knowledge than the best educated adults on Earth. It was an awesome thought. It made him wonder what knowledge was floating around in his parent's heads.

One thing he had really wanted know was what this world was called; or what the symbol for the world was. Tam said it was more of a concept, not a name. But being born and raised on Earth, Carl needed to know names of things. It was really bothering him just to call it "Homeworld." He asked Tam, "what would people from Earth call this planet?" She said, "the closest word in your language which matches how we identify our world, is the word *Earth*."

It made since once he thought about it. We use the

word "Earth" to describe the soil as well as the whole planet. It's kind of our name for *Homeworld*. Earth.

"If it helps," she said, "our scientific name for your planet is Ergrave-411. Named after the scientist who discovered it. But I doubt Earth people would want to rename it; or be referred to as Ergravians. If any of your scientists have discovered our binary star system, or even our planet, I'm sure they've given it a numeric name of some sort."

It was a weird thought. It left Carl confused. Like he had stepped through a mirror, and now stood looking at the reflection which used to be him. *I'm an Ergravian.* He thought. *An Alien.*

He stood in Tam's living room, looking at a picture of Earth displayed on a wall. In each of Tam's rooms there was a *display* wall which looked like a window, but did not look outside. She could display any scene she wanted, from any location. She used these displays to show him different parts of the world. Deserts, ocean, cities. He was surprised to see many cities which looked no more modern than an Earth city. Streets dotted with traffic.

"Not everyone is comfortable with the Displacers," Tam said. "Most people use Hummers or hover cars."

He had not left his grandmother's home since arriving. She had a comfortable bedroom ready for him, with a display window which to his surprise had the same view he saw from the living room window back in Olympia.

"A projection file your mother sent me not long

after they moved in," she said.

It shocked him the first time he walked in. It was so clear it looked like he could step through and be back home. He thought it was a portal of some sort until she explained it.

It made him ache because he knew even if he got back to Earth, he would probably never see that view again. After their first telepathy lesson, Tam realized it bothered him, so she changed it to a mountain scene.

Today she told him she had something special in store. She walked him to the edge of the balcony where he had a clear view of the lake. Earlier there had been people riding Hummers, but now it was quiet.

"Open up," she said. That was how she started a telepathy lesson. It wasn't as intense as when they used the orb, but there was still a lot of information passing back and forth. Much more than could be carried through speech. Receiving thoughts from someone else was much easier than sending; it was just a matter of opening his mind the way he did when he felt peoples feelings.

He cleared his mind, opened up, and reached for Tam's mind. Instantly his head began filling with information.

Rholette.

Hummer.

Willoughby, Arlia, Candy.

Background and details. When he opened his eyes he felt a presence in the room. He turned and saw a short blonde girl standing a few feet behind him, grinning widely. He knew from Tam's telepathed message who this was.

Rholette. She was an old friend of the family. Her father had played with Willoughby when they were young; they had been best friends. Her father's feelings were hurt when Willoughby chose assignment on Earth; he had hoped they would study the wormholes together.

She was Carl's age, and she was here to teach him to use a Hummer. Behind her were two gleaming Hummers propped against the wall. One was a bright metallic blue, about three feet long, which he knew was hers – she had nicknamed it *proton*. Next to it was a dark grey model, six inches shorter. It was a training board; it would not scream across the lake at five hundred miles an hour like in his dream. But even one hundred miles an hour – or twenty knocks as they referred to it here – would be fast enough.

His mind was still *open* from his quick lesson with Tam. Able to send and receive thoughts. Rholette tilted an eyebrow and nodded her head. *You are ready?*

Yes. He thought.

She took a few steps closer and closed her eyes. He did the same. Instantly his head filled with Hummer techniques, skills, and experience. In less than a second he knew enough to operate the board. It had its own power supply, but it was tuned to his brain frequency. He would operate it telepathically the same way he telepathed with Tam. Within five seconds he knew enough to run the Hummer at top speed across land or water. Within ten seconds he could perform tricks. After fifteen seconds he knew something else … but not about the Hummer.

He knew she liked him. He could feel her feelings for him, even though she didn't really know him. And worse yet, as much as he tried to stop feeling it, he liked her too, and he knew she was sensing it.

She was short for her age, a little shorter than Candy, and wore her silken blonde hair in a long ponytail. She had long dark eyelashes and catlike eyes which curved a bit at the ends; almost an oriental look. She didn't only look like a cat, she moved like one too. She wore a skin-tight yellow bodysuit which showed off the lines of muscle in her legs. She was in very good physical condition.

She grabbed the grey board and tossed it to him, then grabbed *proton* and danced out the door. Carl sprinted out behind her. The lighter gravity of this planet made him feel like he could fly on his feet. He could run incredibly fast, but she still sprinted away from him.

When they reached the lake shore, Rholette slid back a small panel at the head of his Hummer; she inserted a key and pressed a button, this was to record Carl's brain frequency and set the board to respond to him. He sent a telepathic message to it; it beeped. Rholette closed the panel and handed him the board. He laid it flat on the shore, stepped onto it and sent a telepathic message.

Up. He said, and the board rose; just inches. He thought of going forward and the board went forward. Sand blew up around him, he had to squint to avoid getting any in his eyes. In seconds he was over the water. The scratchy sand was replaced with the whoosh of moving water. *Faster,* he thought and he was going faster. He turned quickly to the left by leaning his body and thinking of moving. The board bit slightly into the water and kicked up a roostertail which sprayed Rholette who was just a few feet behind him.

Hey!! Rholette filled his head. *You're lucky my hair is tied up mister!* She went flying past him, turned quickly and washed him with a wave. He blinked water out of his eyes and spit a mouthful into the lake. The water tasted peculiar, slightly fruity. He expected his clothes to be soaked, but the pants and shirt Tam had given him shed the water as if they were made of glass. His skin stayed dry.

Faster, and he was flying across the water at almost a hundred miles an hour. The wind blew his hair back and roared in his ears. A couple times Rholette buzzed him, passing on either side at almost twice his speed. Once she washed him out with a wave that knocked him from the board and sent him skipping across the water like a stone – just like a scene from his dream.

I know that lake, she thought to him. He knew what she was talking about. She was seeing his dream, speeding across the lake.

It was real?

It's a real place.

I want to go there.

Maybe some other time, Tam interrupted. Carl looked around but couldn't see her. Fine spray from the boards obscured his view of her house and balcony. *You've got ten minutes,* she continued, *then you need to come back. There are people here who want to meet you.* He felt her knowledge of the people; he knew why they were there and what they

181

wanted with him. It scared him, but excited him at the same time. They were his ticket back to Earth … if he wanted to go back.

He had to admit this *Homeworld* was a fascinating place with a lot of terrific things to see and do. He would love to stay here, but only if his family was with him. Otherwise he needed to be back on Earth, with them.

I need to know why they don't want to come back here, he thought, I need to see it from their point of view.

He wanted to telepath with his parents and understand everything.

Chapter Twenty

It was morning. They had slept in the van in a bakery parking lot. Candy woke to the sound of Willoughby opening the side door. When he saw her, he held up a tray of breakfast muffins, steaming coffee and hot chocolate. He had a thick folded newspaper tucked under one arm. He was looking nervously at Amy who was still sleeping. Candy nudged her awake.

"Oh, chocolate," she said. She gratefully took one of the cups and carefully sipped at the rim of whipped cream, "perfect," she whispered.

Arlia stepped around Willoughby, pulled the newspaper from under his arm and motioned to Amy. "I want a blueberry pastry," she said, "Amy, would you like to come in with me?"

"Sure," Amy set the cup down and rolled out of the Van.

Candy looked at Amy, then at Willoughby. She knew something was up. Amy was from a messed up household so she probably did not recognize the *I want to talk to you alone* signs, but Candy spotted them, and she was immediately curious. Why would Mom want to talk to Amy alone? What was going on? She locked eyes with Willoughby and he gave her the *I'll tell you later,* look.

Arlia stopped Amy just before they stepped into the bakery. There was a concrete bench by the door, surrounded by flowering plants which were near the end of their season. "There's something in the paper this morning you need to read," she sat down and folded the paper open to an article and Amy's seventh grade class picture:

OLYMPIA: The case of a 13-year old Olympia girl, missing since a daring daylight kidnapping in front of her home this week, took a bizarre twist yesterday when police arrested her Uncle, Emmett Nottingham. Police spokespeople said an exhaustive investigation had discovered Nottingham to be the girl's biological father, formerly known as Harlan Nottingham. Nottingham and his wife Patricia disappeared without explanation nine years ago from their home in Astoria, Oregon. Nottingham, who then identified himself in court records as her Uncle and designated legal guardian, moved to Olympia shortly thereafter. Police are questioning Nottingham as to the whereabouts of his wife. "Foul play in her disappearance has not been ruled out," Police spokeswoman Kristin Phaulk said, "at this time we're still trying to piece together the details." Police are pursing persons of interest in the kidnapping but are not yet releasing names. They say the Father is currently not a suspect in his daughter's disappearance.

"Wow," Amy whispered. She handed the paper back to Arlia.

"Amy," Arlia said, "Willoughby and I don't know what your situation was at home … but if you want to go back, we'll understand." She put her arm around Amy and gave her a motherly hug. Neither spoke for a moment.

"They think he killed my Mom?" Amy asked.

"Well," Arlia said, "it sounds like they're just questioning him about what happened to her. Maybe it was just a bad breakup. Maybe she left him suddenly, so he changed his name and ran off with you so she couldn't find you."

Amy perked up. "You think so? You think my Mom might be out there somewhere looking for me?"

"Anything is possible I guess," Arlia said, "but Willoughby and I are concerned. We understand if you want to go back, but we don't want to send you back into a situation where you're going to get hurt."

Amy looked down, almost embarrassed. "It was nothing like that – I mean – he never hit me. He was just … well … never very nice. Always, angry or depressed or just … empty. It's like," she looked up at the sky, as if looking for what she wanted to say, "what we're doing right now, I should probably feel afraid, or homesick. But I don't. Because home never felt like a real home. It was just a depressing place that I couldn't wait to get away from."

"I see," Arlia said. Her face gave away the sadness she felt when she thought of Amy's life with her Uncle …

185

Father.

"So ... no, I don't want to go back. But I'd like to know what happened."

"Well, I'm sure when the truth comes out it will make the papers. We can find out then."

"Thank you Missus Tennison. I know I haven't thanked you or Mister Tennison for bringing me with you. I'm glad I'm here."

"Well Amy, we're glad you're here too. We really are," she slapped her hands on her knees and started to stand up. "Now, we're going to have to see about changing your look a little so you don't look so much like that picture," she pointed to the newspaper. "You have such beautiful long hair too. How do you feel about short hair."

Amy cringed. "I could live with it, I guess."

"Maybe just for a while? Until we see how things are going to turn out?"

"Okay," Amy's voice was small. She was giving in, but she wasn't completely happy about it. "So long as Candy doesn't tease me."

"I think I can promise that," Arlia said, "Oh ... and you probably don't need to call me Missus Tennison. For appearances sake would you feel okay calling me Mom?"

Amy smiled, "Mom? Sure! Wow, I've got a Mom!" She grabbed the newspaper from Arlia and ran back to the Van where she huddled in the back with Candy and read the article to her.

Arlia nodded to Willoughby. They were in a small town, probably not a big risk of someone spotting Amy.

But before the end of the day they would be in Crescent City, California; she would need to have her new look by then. "Find me a drugstore," she said as they climbed into the van.

"We tracked James Morlana," the girl said. She was fourteen, on Earth she had been a high school student, but here she piloted a starship. "It's not good. Tennison sent him to the same place she sent the NSA agents."

"And?" the project commander asked.

"They've got him."

"Blast it!" he spat. "Well ... notify the ground people. We've got a bigger problem now than the Tennison's running. We need some damage control."

"Do we pull him out?"

"No ... not right away. Let's wait and see what they do with him. But keep a lock on him just in case. Maybe they can lead US for a while the same way they've been trying to get us to lead them."

Chapter Twenty One

There were four men and two women on the balcony when Carl returned to Tam's house. Rholette was following close behind him.

"These are people from the Research council," Tam said, "will you feel comfortable telepathing with us?"

"Sure," Carl said. He was afraid he sounded too eager; too much like a little kid. He opened up and immediately they were communicating with him. It came like pings. Like seeds of information sprouting into a mental language. They were all communicating with him – and with each other – at almost the same time. Yesterday it would have been too much for him to handle, but today it was okay.

There were quick introductions. The two women were Lhoree and Robenga. Three of the men were Protega, Emeel, and Shell. The fourth man did not have a name, he used a symbol. In his case Carl noticed a lot of extra information floating around the 'pings' of communication. His only way of communicating was through telepathy, he couldn't speak. He was not from this planet, nor from Carl's planet. He was from a desert world even further away from here than Earth. Carl caught glimpses of the man's upbringing. Hot, dry sands and strange creatures. Carl reached, trying to learn more, it seemed very interesting. Then suddenly the man shut off his mind, his eyebrows curled as if Carl had just said something wrong. The others glanced at him briefly but did not stop their discussion.

They wanted to know if Carl wanted to return to Earth. If he did, they had information for him to pass on to his parents. It took no time at all for Carl to make up his mind; he wanted to return. And the great thing was, due to the telepathic connection, he did not have to explain to them why. They could feel it, and understand it, exactly the way Carl felt it and understood it. It was such a relief to be able to communicate this way, it totally lacked the frustration that so often came with speech.

Instantly they began feeding him information. Speeches, notes, arguments to persuade Willoughby and Arlia to return; almost bribery. And something else which Carl found interesting, and comforting: instructions for continuing their lives on Earth if they decided not to leave.

So we can stay and not be chased forever, he thought.

His head filled with information while his thoughts drifted to Candy, and Mom and Dad, and getting back. Splitting his thoughts this way was a trick Tam had taught him. She said it would keep him from being overwhelmed by all the ideas his head would fill with during telepathy. It was like having two separate brains in his head.

Tam said people on Earth used this *second brain* trick all the time but didn't know they were doing it, and because of that they could never learn to do it right. At best a person would think they were going crazy if they knew they did it.

Carl had learned that the brain was a huge instrument with almost unlimited ability, and humans were wasting it. Like living in a huge mansion and never coming out of a small bedroom.

"You get so used to hearing with your ears, and seeing with your eyes," Tam said, "that you never try to see and hear with your mind."

"Why didn't Mom and Dad try to teach us this?" he asked.

"You'll find out when you get back," she said. "Telepathically, Earth can be a very noisy place. Imagine a room of deaf people, all making sounds with their vocal chords, but because they can't hear it, they don't know they're doing it. That's what Earth is like for a telepath. You'll need to learn to tune things out before you can tune anything in." Carl remembered his Dad saying something about that right after they left Olympia.

Eventually the Research Council left, and plans were made; much more quickly than he had expected. He had hoped to stay a little longer. He had seen much of the planet through Tam's projection walls, but he wanted to see it in person. He wanted to feel the wind blowing and smell the air. He had not yet walked the streets of a city.

And the lake from his dream – which Rholette said was real. He *had* to see it.

Rholette! He turned around, she was still there. Leaning lazily against the balcony, looking at him as if she had been waiting for him to say something.

She spoke out loud, "Well … just met, and now you're leaving," she looked genuinely sad, "you're an interesting guy Carl, I had hoped we could be friends." The translator was still in his ear, he was listening to the English translation, but he realized he could also understand the native language coming from her lips. Not all of it, but enough to understand what she was saying. He had picked it up during the telepathy lessons.

"I know," he said, "me too," and he meant it. During the bond with Rholette, when she had been teaching him to ride the Hummer, he had felt himself becoming attached to her; almost as if the Hummer lessons had been a series of dates. He liked her, and he knew from communicating with her that she was a good person, a smart person, fun to be with … and she liked him too. "You ever think of applying for an Earth assignment?"

"You don't have Hummers on Earth, do you?" she asked.

"No," he said sadly.

She grinned sadly, "I'm too much of a Hummer junkie to give it up."

Tam *pinged* Carl's mind. *Earth's not ready for Hummers. But you'll be taking one back with you.*

"Huh?" he said out loud.

"You'll be taking a Hummer back with you," she

191

said, "but under strict conditions."

"Why?"

"We don't know where your parents are. But they probably didn't sit and wait for you to come back. We'll put you back where you came from, and you'll need a way to get around. The Hummer is the best tool for that." He wasn't about to argue with her. The idea of buzzing along the freeway on a Hummer was exciting. "But you'll get a modified model. Like a normal one it will only react to your brain frequency. But if it becomes damaged in any way – like someone opening it up to see how it works – it will dissolve away just like the paper water cups."

He was suspicious. He remembered the small dime-sized tracking device which had been stuck under the station wagon. Tam felt this concern.

"It won't track you," she said, "but even if it did, we have no way to know when you've contacted your parents. And when you do I'm sure they'll scan the board for a tracking signal." She turned, walked over to a cabinet and dug through a drawer. "There's something I want you to give your mother," she said, "from me." She turned around and walked back to Carl. She handed him a small doll. It was about six inches long, with blonde hair, blue eyes and a green dress which looked hand made. "Your mother made it when she was a little girl. I imagine she would like to have it. Maybe even pass it on to Candy."

Tam's eyes were sad. She was a wonderful grand-mother; she had been helpful and understanding. All she wanted was to see her daughter and her grandchildren. She had learned a lot about Candy from telepathing with

Carl. But it wasn't as good as seeing someone standing in front of you … or giving a daughter and granddaughter a hug.

He put his arms around her and hugged her. "Thank you grandma," he said. He wasn't quite sure what he was thanking her for, but she seemed to know. She hugged him back.

Chapter Twenty Two

Carl's mind was telepathically *open* when he reappeared at the snack kiosk at the rest area along the freeway. He had a Hummer tucked under his arm and a new blue backpack slung over his shoulder.

It hit him like a punch in the face. Deafening white noise. The mental voices of billions of people who didn't know they were sending their thoughts. And along with it came feelings; every possible feeling people could have: happiness, agony, anger, jealousy, disappointment, every feeling came crashing down on him like a load of rocks. He dropped to his knees and pressed his hands to his ears, but it didn't stop.

Blank … blank … blank … he thought. And the voices faded.

When he finally opened his eyes he was on hands and knees, staring at the ground. His knees hurt from dropping so quickly onto the pavement. The Hummer had fallen into the grass, his backpack was hanging off his elbow. All it contained was the doll for his mother. He had left behind the clothes Tam had given him, and changed back into his normal Earth clothes.

The sun was already behind the hills, it was early evening. He wasn't exactly sure what he should do first; start moving, or try to reach his parents telepathically. He didn't really want to open up again right away, not after the noise he just went through. He understood why his parents didn't use it.

Tam had advised him to reach out for Amy. He knew her, he had tapped her feelings before, in the car. Through her feelings he might be able to trace a direction. He had heard his parents talking about the Redwood Highway, so that's the way he would follow.

He reached into his pockets, everything was the same as it had been when he left here, including enough change in his pockets to get some chips and a pop.

Arlia almost choked on her hamburger. They were in a small fast-food restaurant in Crescent City, California, across the street from the motel where they were registered for the night.

She spit her hamburger out and coughed a couple times, someone was holding a glass of water in front of her but she didn't see them. Her eyes were wide, staring at nothing. Her mind was suddenly back in Oregon.

"I felt him," she whispered. Tears were welling up in her eyes, "he's back."

"But how …." Willoughby began.

"He's telepath now," Arlia said. She had felt nothing more than a 'ping' of sensation as Carl reappeared on Earth, and when he tuned the world out the feeling faded. But the ping had carried a lot with it. "He's been with Tam," she said.

"How do you know?" Candy asked. "Can you talk to him?"

"No," Arlia said, "I felt him just for a second. I think he knows which direction we've gone. He'll get closer, then we'll try to find him."

"I miss Carl," Amy said. She had been sitting quietly in the booth – sandwiched between Candy and Arlia – silently chewing greasy french fries and sipping a chocolate milkshake. Her hair was chopped short, but styled well. She looked good. They had added a little red tint to it too. She looked nothing like her seventh grade class picture.

She looks like she should be in a band, Candy thought.

Arlia was looking at Willoughby, "he has a message," she said.

Willoughby nodded. But Candy wasn't satisfied with that. "A message? What message? Like from the Homeworld? Like return or die?"

Willoughby grinned, "nothing so severe I imagine. Either a request for us to return, or permission to stay, or they're just going to track him until he finds us, then grab us all at once." He looked at Arlia, expecting her to say something.

"I don't care," Candy said. This surprised everyone. "I don't care where we live. Washington, California,

Denmark, or another planet. But we shouldn't be separated again," her eyes were filling with tears, "we shouldn't."

Arlia hugged her. "I agree."

Candy wiped a tear away. She was afraid for Carl. She didn't like the idea of him out there all alone in the dark, no one to help him. No one to be brave for. *I'll be brave for you Carl,* she thought. *Please just hurry and get here.*

A big truck blew its air-horn as Carl buzzed past it in the dark. He doubted the driver would tell anyone he had been passed by a teenager on a skateboard doing a hundred miles an hour. Who would believe something like that?

Carl finished the last chip, then crumpled the empty bag and stuffed it in his pocket. As he turned onto a straight stretch he brought the Hummer's speed up to around one hundred fifty, then took a big drink of pop. With his knees bent slightly, one hand out for balance, the other tipping the can to his lips, and his hair blowing back in the wind, he looked like a one of those *extreme sports* guys from the TV commercials.

The Hummer had built-in safeguards to prevent the operator from running into large objects: like cliffs, big rocks, trees, and in Carl's case … traffic. It also had an energy deflector which kept him from getting hit by road debris, like bugs, rocks, even deer, or birds. Without it he wouldn't dare go so fast.

The trees closed in as the road narrowed and he approached a tight fifty mile per hour corner. As he entered it, he swung the board, brought it up almost com-

197

pletely sideways and rode the corner at over a hundred. It was a total rush! He leaned slightly forward and telepathed the board to increase speed. On Earth it was harder to operate the board telepathically when he had to block out all the noise too. Kind of like a basketball player trying to shoot a free throw while people are throwing things. But Tam had been a good teacher. She had known what he would need here.

Even though he was all alone and did not know exactly where Candy and his parents were, he felt comfortable; confident that he could track them down. Even Siberia would have been a comfortable place right now. Anyplace, so long as it was on planet Earth, third planet from Sol. *His* Homeworld. The Hummer could get him home from anywhere on the planet. He grinned. Just the thought of buzzing across an ocean on the Hummer. Breezing past a cruise ship, waving at wide-eyed passengers. Slowing enough for dolphins to swim next to him. Riding up a twenty-foot swell at three hundred miles an hour, going airborne for a hundred yards before leveling out over the water.

Could he ride through a hurricane? Would the deflectors work as stabilizers to keep him from being blown off? His dad would know.

He was heading over a series of tall hills. As the road rose he could feel the temperature dip a few degrees. In the dark stretches between lights he could barely see the road at all. Just faint white dashes in a sea of black. But the board was instructed to keep him over pavement, so he didn't have to worry about running off the road.

Sometimes the trees would clear away and he could see down into a valley which stretched for miles. Lights twinkled in the distance.

He crossed the summit of a hill and the road curved and dipped down steeply. He felt the board follow it. He bent his legs slightly to ride the corner.

It happened too fast for him to react; but the board reacted. The corner was tight, and he was travelling very fast; over a hundred. Suddenly headlights flashed in front of him; a big pickup truck with oversized tires, speeding up the summit in the wrong lane. A drunk driver.

The board went from over a hundred miles an hour to zero in just seconds. Carl would have been pitched forward directly into the grill of the truck but the board went vertical like a wall in front of him. It pushed him upward so fast the wind was knocked out of him. He heard a cry come from his mouth as all the air in his lungs was forced out. The truck sped by beneath him and vanished around the corner, lost in the dark again. With the danger gone, the board slowly floated to the ground, stopping about six inches from the pavement.

Carl couldn't take a breath. He felt like he had been crushed between two boulders. His chest was screaming. Every nerve in him was hurting. All he wanted to do was breathe, but he was afraid his lungs had collapsed.

I'm going to die, he thought. Then his lungs convulsed, sucking in a big breath. It hurt, but he couldn't stop it. He exhaled, then inhaled again. Then began gasping as if he had just run a mile. Well, his hurricane question had been answered. The board would take measures to keep him from falling off. But he questioned whether it was worth the pain.

"No hurricane riding," he whispered to the night. It was several minutes before he felt well enough to move again.

Chapter Twenty Three

James Morlana's seat had no window. He had no idea where he was. Thankfully the plane was finally landing. It was the first time he had ever flown, and he didn't like it. Too much bumping, and up and down, and this way and that. He felt lucky he had not thrown up … yet.

Across from him were three men with guns. They never spoke a word, just watched him. One of them had taken the Displacer when James got on the plane. The moment the man touched it, it turned to dust.

So much for a rescue, James thought, now that they have nothing to track me with.

The plane was dropping rapidly; too rapidly he thought, even though he had no experience to judge it. It bumped hard when it hit the runaway, then the nose dipped and the engines screamed as the plane quickly slowed to a stop.

Almost immediately the door was being opened and other people were coming in. A parade of people. Men and women, short and tall, some dressed like business-men, some wearing tee shirts and jeans. All of them looked at him suspiciously as they passed.

A woman in a business suit stepped into the plane. She looked like someone who could work with his mother at the insurance office in Olympia. She had long dark hair and was quite tall. She spotted him the moment she stepped in, and kept her eyes on him as she approached. She extended her hand, "James? I'm Jessica Sharpe, it's nice to meet you." James shook her hand. She had a firm grip. Her hand was warm and dry. She pointed to the seat belts, "you can get out that if you want." He unbuck-led, but not without keeping an eye on the men with the guns. For a moment he was afraid they would start shoot-ing the minute he was unbuckled. The metal clasp clicked, the belt fell away, but the men did not move. It was a small freedom, but at this point he welcomed every little thing.

"Where are my parents?" he asked. He wanted more than anything to see them step onto the plane right now, come over and hug him and tell him everything was fine. He had felt so grown up when he was given the task to approach Carl and the Tennisons. Given a Displacer and told how to use it. He wondered how Carl was doing. If he was mad at being sent to the Homeworld? How could he be mad? Mad about being able to travel to another planet? James would give anything to trade places with him right now. Ever since he learned the truth about his parents and where they were from, he wanted to visit the Homeworld. But now, here he was. Wherever *here* was.

"We don't know where your parents are," Jessica said. "When we get inside and get settled you can try calling them."

She led him out of the plane. The sun was very bright; and hot. Everything looked barren. The runway was flat, the distance was blurred by the watery wave of heat rising from the ground. In the far distance rose tall mountains, brown and barren. Everything was brown. To the left were a series of dull concrete buildings. To the right were airplane hangars covered with brown camouflage webbing so they couldn't be spotted from the air.

"This way," Jessica said, leading him toward the concrete blockhouses. There were soldiers there, dressed in brown and green combat fatigues; they were all carrying guns. Two soldiers opened a thick steel door in the building. Inside was complete darkness; as if he were about to step into a hole and fall to the center of the Earth.

When they reached the doorway, one of the soldiers stopped him. James turned to look for Ms. Sharpe. She was standing a few feet back talking to two men in suits and sunglasses. One of them was talking on a cellphone.

"Pull out of the area," she was saying to the man on the phone, "this has priority now. All we're doing out there is chasing them away," she glanced at James, "let's see what we can do with him, and go from there."

Do with him? What did that mean? It sounded too much like his biology instructor talking about the frogs they were about to cut open. It didn't sound good.

"This way James," she said. She turned him back

toward the dark doorway and guided him.

He stepped into the oily black of the bunker. The soldiers closed the door behind him. Jessica stayed outside for a moment, still talking to the man on the cellphone.

"Make sure the records are adjusted," she said, "and I want a priority put on bringing his parents in. Let me know when everything is taken care of. As far as the outside world knows, James Morlana doesn't exist. He never existed. He's ours now."

Chapter Twenty Four

Candy couldn't sleep. The moment Carl had vanished from that rest area her life had turned dark and serious. And now, knowing he was on his way back, she felt something she had never felt before. The fear of losing him again.

The highway between here and there had seemed narrow and dark. Like something out of an old medieval fantasy novel. Surrounded by forest inhabited with trolls and dragons and giant snakes waiting to eat someone like Carl.

She was afraid for him. He was out there alone, trying to find his way back. Alone in the dark on that highway. She knew how she would feel if it were her out there; she would be terrified.

The board slowed. Carl could see nothing. He knew the two-lane highway was about a foot beneath him. He knew tall trees bordered either side of the road. But he could see nothing. The sky was overcast, blocking the stars and any hope of even a sliver of moonlight. Even when he did manage to see something around him, it was only fog, moving around him like a ghost. Sometimes something dark would grow out of it, and it would startle him until he realized it was only a tree.

The board drifted left, and Carl heard something moving on the pavement nearby; a cautious tapping. A deer? A mountain lion? Bigfoot? It could be anything.

A shiver went down his spine. Partially from cold, and partially from fear of whatever was out there in the dark. Whatever dangers lurked out there, the board would avoid them. Although it probably couldn't do much if something with strong legs and sharp teeth decided to lunge suddenly at him.

He tried not to think about it. He stretched his mind again. Not opening it completely, but enough to look for Amy. His parents wouldn't risk broadcasting their position; and somehow he knew his mother was aware he was back.

He thought he had found Amy earlier. He could feel her friendship with Candy. A deep friendship, appreciation, and personal bond. They were best friends. It was easy to find because no one else in this part of the country would be carrying such a strong emotional imprint of his sister. As he reached for her, he could almost sense her calling him, giving him directions. It was soothing. Much better than just staring into the darkness waiting for something to leap out.

Amy was dreaming deeply. She was standing in a pitch black cave. There had been lights, but now they were gone. She was lost. Alone.

"Amy?" a voice called from far away. It echoed through the cave. It was Carl.

"Carl?" she called out. "Carl! I'm here!"

"Where?" the voice was still far away, but louder.

"I'm here!"

"Keep talking!"

"I'm over here! Follow my voice! I'm over here!" There was another sound near her. Mumbling. It was Candy's parents. She couldn't see them, but she could *feel* them. She could not understand what they were saying.

"Amy!" Carl continued to call out.

"Yes! Carl! Over here!"

They wanted to call Carl too, but they couldn't. There were other people out there. People looking for them. People who would recognize their voices and come get them.

"Carl! I'm here! Can you hear me?"

"Yes, Amy. I can hear you … keep talking.! He was getting closer. There was light coming with his voice. She could see a faint glow ahead of her in the dark, beginning to illuminate the cave around her. She turned around to look at the Tennisons. They were standing just a couple feet behind her, their arms around each other. They were crying.

"Thank you Amy," Arlia whispered. "Thank you."

Chapter Twenty Five

Sometime during the night Candy finally dozed off. Her dreams were wild images, bits and pieces, Carl on vacation, Amy in her garden, Tami Seltzer on a computer trying to find them while a green-scaled alien stood behind her holding a mind-ray. She dreamed she was awake and the night was never ending. Carl was snatched off the highway by a tentacled tree which dropped him into a bottomless pit.

She was sharing a room with Amy. Her parents were next door. They didn't have a connecting door, but the walls were thin enough to hear everything.

She woke to the sound of knocking. At first she thought it was her door. Then she realized it was her parent's room. It woke Amy too. They sat up, listening. They heard the door open, then Arlia scream and cry.

Tears filled Candy's eyes before she was even out of the bed. "Amy! Amy! He's back!" she ran out in her tee shirt and shorts.

Carl was standing just inside the door, Arlia's arms were wrapped around him, she was crying as if he had just returned from the dead. Willoughby was standing next to her, trying to be calm, but he kept wiping his eyes.

Candy was in Carl's arms before he was even completely turned around. She tried to talk, but nothing came out of her mouth except whining and sobbing. He lifted her off the floor and spun her around.

"I'm surprised to find you here," he teased, "I expected you to still be at the rest area … looking in the mirror."

She wiped her eyes, "funny," she said.

Amy poked her head in the door. Carl smiled, she smiled back. "Oh my," he said, "you've joined a band!"

She rubbed a hand through her hair. "Your Mom did it. You think it looks okay?"

"It's … great," he said, "I mean … you look like a high school student."

She looked away, embarrassed, "thanks."

He turned back to his parents, "I don't even know where to begin," he looked at his mother, "grandma says hi," he turned back to Candy, "she says hi to you too. Says to come visit her sometime."

The room got quiet. Carl looked a little embarrassed. Willoughby pointed to the Hummer, leaning against the wall by the door. "I see you've been having fun. I used to ride one of those."

"My gosh Dad, it's incredible! I learned on the same lake you did. Jhonnia's daughter Rholette taught me … they say hi, by the way."

209

"Jhonnia … " Willoughby smiled, "it's been a long time."

Carl noticed his mother looking suspiciously at the Hummer. "They promised they're not tracking me," Carl said. "Oh yeah …" he slung the backpack off his shoulder and unzipped it. He was grinning. "Grandma told me to give you this," he pulled out the doll.

Fresh tears poured down Arlia's cheeks, "oh my," she said. She slowly shook her head and wiped her eyes. "Years ago I told her to keep it, because … because I wanted to give it to my daughter one day," she handed it to Candy. "Here you go dear. I think you'll like it … it … keeps bad dreams away." She was crying and smiling and laughing all at the same time. Candy looked a little wary, but she took the doll.

"They want me to make you an offer," Carl continued, he paused, looking nervously between his parents. This was a weird situation for him, making demands of his parents. Or it felt that way anyway. He had been gone barely a day, but he felt years older; like an eternity had passed. It was great to see his family again, but at the same time they seemed different. Of course it wasn't they who were different, it was him.

"I know," Willoughby said, "they want us to come back."

"Well … sorta. They say they would prefer us to come back, but they're willing to give you a reassignment to another city if you insist on staying here. If you want to stay on Earth but don't want reassignment, they ask that you remember your oath not to share technology with

Earth, and …" he looked at his mother, "they want you to send the Displacer back."

Arlia looked at Willoughby. Giving up the Displacer was very permanent. Very final. It was also their only dependable line of defense. "I don't even know where to send it," she said.

Carl pulled something out of his back pocket. It looked like a pocket calculator, about half the size of Arlia's Displacer, and half as thick. "They gave me this. To either take us back, or to send your Displacer and the Hummer back." He looked sadly at the Hummer. It would be painful to give it up.

Arlia took the device from Carl's hand, turned it over and examined it. "Wow," she said, "they've come a long way."

"So what are we going to do?" Carl asked.

Willoughby and Arlia exchanged glances. "Now that you've been there Carl," Arlia said, "can you understand why we don't want to go back? Why we like it better here?"

"Not completely," he said, "but I can, if you'll let me." His parents knew what he meant. A telepathic bond. "I'm not sure I would want to live there," he continued, "but I would sure like to be able to visit now and then."

"Well," Arlia said, looking at her husband, "how do we accept reassignment?"

"We go back and tell them," Carl said. "And while we're there, I can teach Candy to ride a Hummer."

Candy's eyes perked up. Amy stepped around from behind her. "You mean I can go too? To another world?"

Arlia sighed. Willoughby put his arms around her. Carl stepped over to them. He opened his mind, fighting to block out the noise of humanity. His parents opened up as well and for an instant which passed too quickly for Candy or Amy to notice, they exchanged all the information Carl had about his trip. Including Tam and Rholette, and the Research Council. On Carl's end, he grasped glimpses inside his parent's minds. Their love for each other, and their perception of him as *son*. It was a weird sensation. It cast a light on their 'parental' overprotective behavior. He used to think they didn't give him the freedom he deserved as a teenager. But now he saw it the way they saw it; protection. He saw the tiny baby, lying wrapped in a blanket, not able to take care of itself at all. It was him. Carl as an infant. Then taking his first steps, still needing help to stand. First day at school, a little boy looking up into his parent's eyes, terrified of being away from them. And the ache they felt as he walked through those doors and out of their sight. Tears rolling from their eyes as they felt him growing up. A feeling of pride and of loss. With each day he grew a little further away from them, and they began to feel a little more alone.

And there was more. A wisdom. Perhaps just a feeling which came with age. They had more years behind them. A year to him was an eternity; to them it was a blip on a screen. They had a more patient view of life than he did. They could see how it flowed like a river; taking a certain course before pouring into the ocean or evaporating into the air. But he could only see it from the shore where he stood. And around the next bend it vanished.

He saw his mother's fear. Fear that they would not be allowed back on Earth once they left. Fear that she would be forced to live on a world where her thoughts were not her own; where nothing was private. She enjoyed the mental solitude of Earth. The fact that people could not read each other's minds. She preferred the sound of the word "Rose" to the quick image of a rose flashing into her mind. She liked keeping her thoughts to herself. She was even feeling uncomfortable about opening up her thoughts to him right now.

All of that came to him in the blink of an eye. A seed which grew in his mind.

"Let me check us out of the motel," Willoughby said, "and move the van somewhere where it will be safe until we get back."

Arlia's eyes were closed, her head was down. Candy and Amy were obviously excited, practically busting.

Willoughby and Carl looked at each other. They said nothing. Eventually Willoughby nodded and headed out the door. Carl understood. Everything was different now. But everything was going to be alright.

He flipped open the cover of the Displacer. It was already set for Tam's living room. Carl hoped she wasn't alone.

Rholette sat at the edge of the lake. A couple kids were running Hummers across the water. There was a bit of a wind, making the water choppy. She had been watching puffs of clouds drift over, seeing images in them. But now her gaze was on the distant balcony of Tam's house. She looked over there all the time, expecting ... hoping ... to see Carl standing there smiling at her.

Tam walked to the edge of the balcony. It was too far away to really see her face. Rholette waved, Tam waved back.

Around the corner of the house, where the steps led from the balcony down to the shore, Rholette saw three figures emerge from Tam's house. Two girls carrying small Hummers came running toward her. One looked kind of like Tam. Behind them was a boy ...

Rholette leaped to her feet and ran toward him. She didn't care about the puffs of clouds anymore. She was on one.

Homeworld: Book Two

Alien Among Us

coming Summer 2000

James sat up slowly, still tired. He blinked a couple times and shook his head to make sure he wasn't still dreaming. He wasn't alone in his dark little cell anymore. Sitting a few feet away, looking at him with silly grins on their faces, were Carl and Candy Tennison.

"Ohmygod!" he shouted. He jumped to his feet and rushed into their arms. It was unbelievable. Of all the people to join him here, his best friend. "But how …"

"Answers later," Carl said. "Right now we have to get out of here."

James was so excited he was shaking. "You have a Displacer?"

"Well," Carl glanced at Candy, "No."

"But … how did you get in here?"

"Same way you did," Carl said, "we let ourselves get captured." He looked up at the thick frosted glass on the window.

James lowered his eyes. His euphoria was fading quickly. No miraculous escape, just two friends in the same boat. Still ... if he was going to be here, it felt good to have friends. "No use going out the window. It looks like there are bars on the other side."

Carl looked at Candy as if he was speaking, but said nothing. She nodded and stepped over to the window.

James decided that he was either still dreaming, or he had gone insane. Candy Tennison ... little Candy ... Carl's little sister who James teased and taunted, stepped over to the window, smashed her fist through the glass, then grabbed one of the iron bars and pulled it out of the cement casing. Carl and James covered their eyes as fragments of cement and glass showered the cell. James' jaw dropped open. Candy grabbed another bar and ripped it out. And as if that wasn't freaky enough, her face started to change. Within seconds she wasn't Candy Tennison anymore.

About the Author

Casey Lytle was born on planet Earth in the early 1960's. He's been spilling strange stories out of his head since he was ten years old. Although he worked as a computer programmer, he was very bad at it, and chose to chase a writing career instead.

He has two incredible daughters who are terrific writers and served as editors for Alien in the Mirror.

Casey hopes to one day spend the night in an orbiting space hotel, and eventually be the first modern human buried on Mars. When his mind is not wandering to far-away places, it is planted on terra firma in the Pacific Northwest.